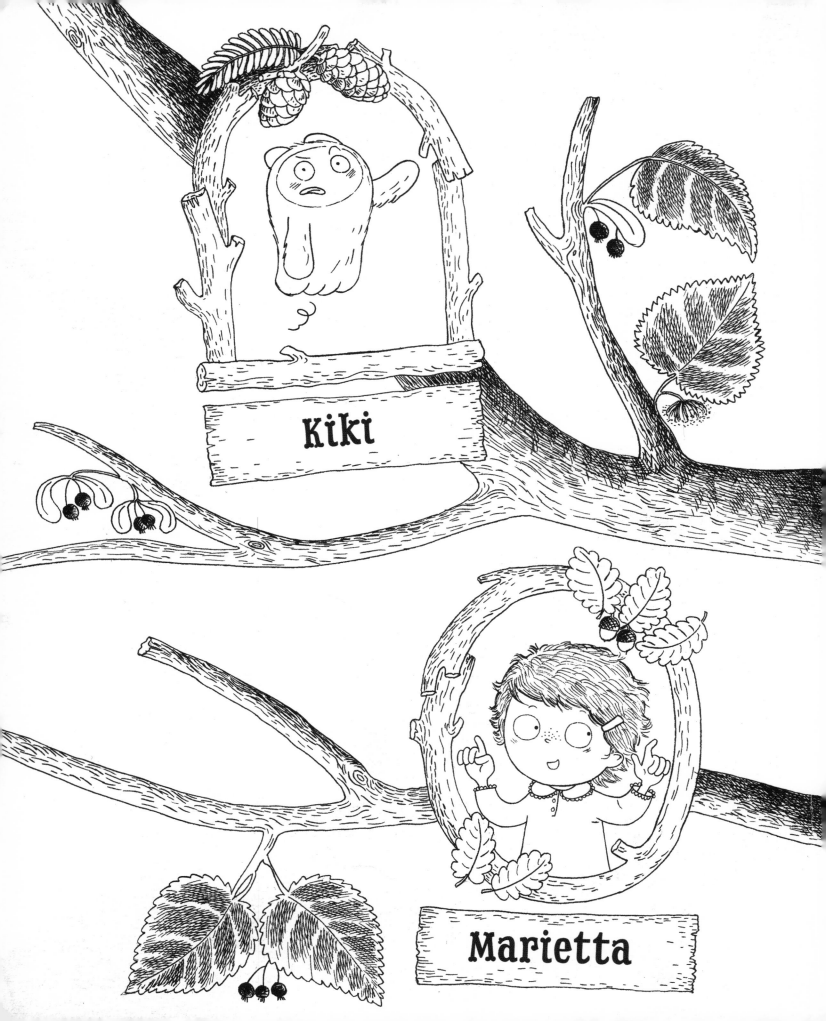

Kiki

Marietta

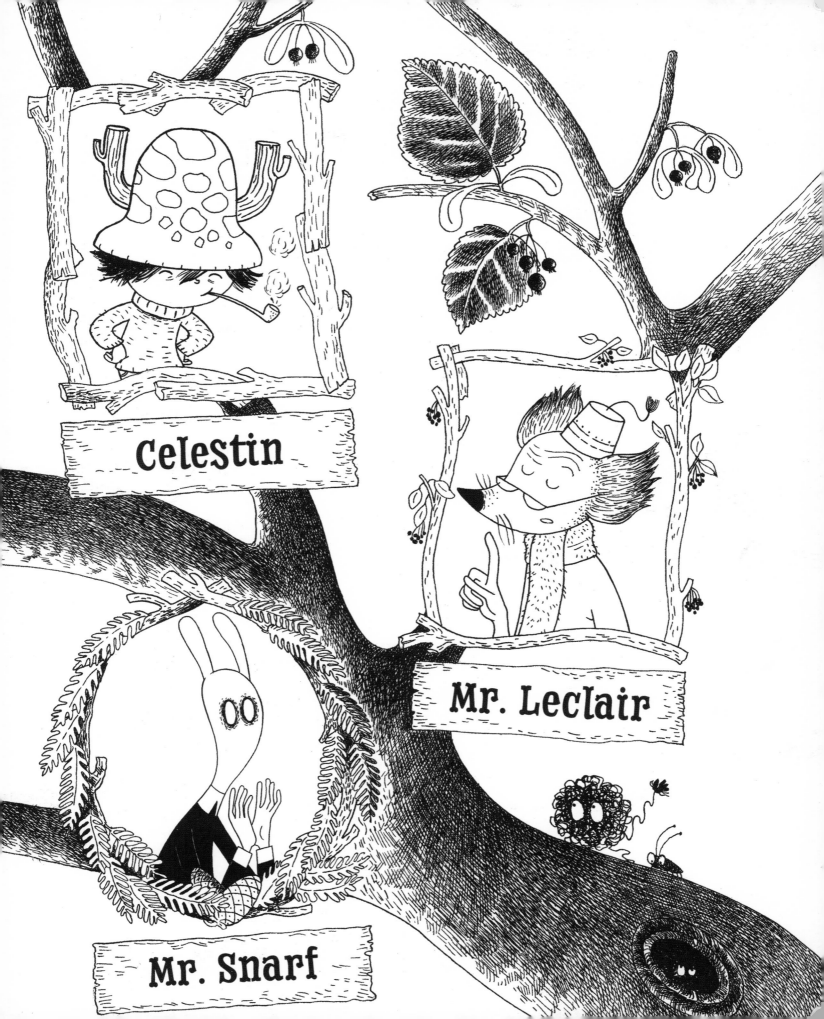

Celestin

Mr. Leclair

Mr. Snarf

HOTEL STRANGE

#1

Wake Up, Spring

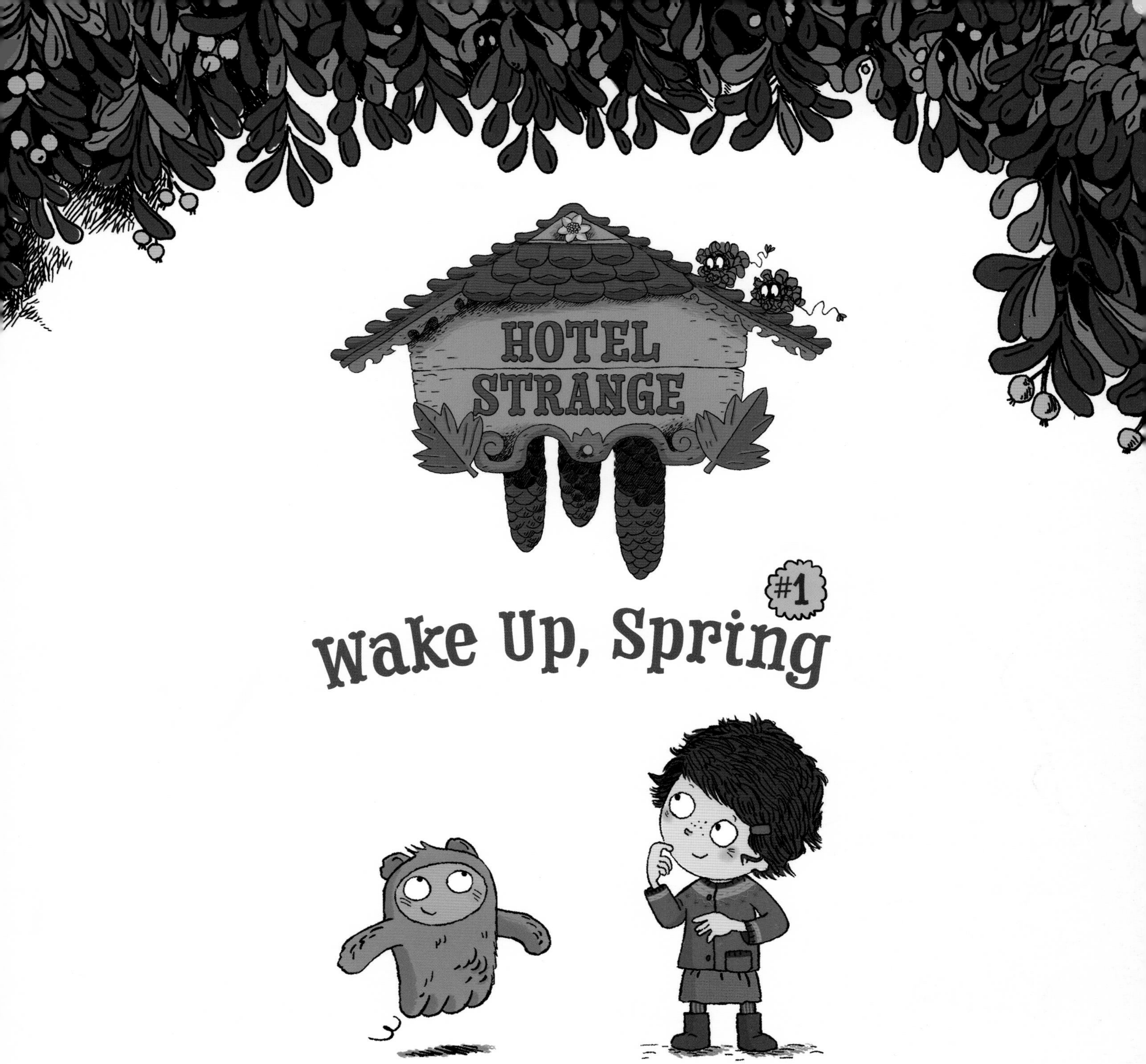

Florian and Katherine Ferrier
illustrations and coloring by Katherine Ferrier

Graphic Universe™ • Minneapolis

Story by Florian and Katherine Ferrier
Illustrations and coloring by Katherine Ferrier
Translation by Carol Burrell

This work received the support of La Cité internationale de la bande dessinée et de l'image (comics museum, library, and arts complex) through an author residency at La maison des auteurs in Angoulême, France.

First American edition published in 2015 by Graphic Universe™

Graphic Universe™
A division of Lerner Publishing Group, Inc.
241 First Avenue North
Minneapolis, MN 55401 USA

For reading levels and more information, look up this title at www.lernerbooks.com.

Main body text set in Andy Std 11/12. Typeface provided by Monotype.

Library of Congress Cataloging-in-Publication Data

Ferrier, Florian, author.
    Wake up, spring / by Florian and Katherine Ferrier ; illustrations and coloring by Katherine Ferrier ; translation by Carol Burrell.
        pages cm. — (Hotel Strange)
    Summary: Although it is spring, the winter weather will not end and the quirky residents of Hotel Strange decide to find out for themselves where Mr. Springtime has gone.
    ISBN 978-1-4677-8584-6 (lb : alk. paper)
    ISBN 978-1-4677-8648-5 (pb : alk. paper)
    ISBN 978-1-4677-8855-7 (eb pdf)
    I. Graphic novels. [1. Graphic novels. 2. Seasons—Fiction.]
    I. Ferrier, Katherine, author, illustrator. II. Burrell, Carol Klio, translator. III. Title.
PZ7.7.F48Wak 2015
741.5'973—dc23   2015000711

Manufactured in the United States of America
1 – VP – 7/15/15

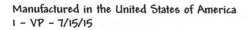

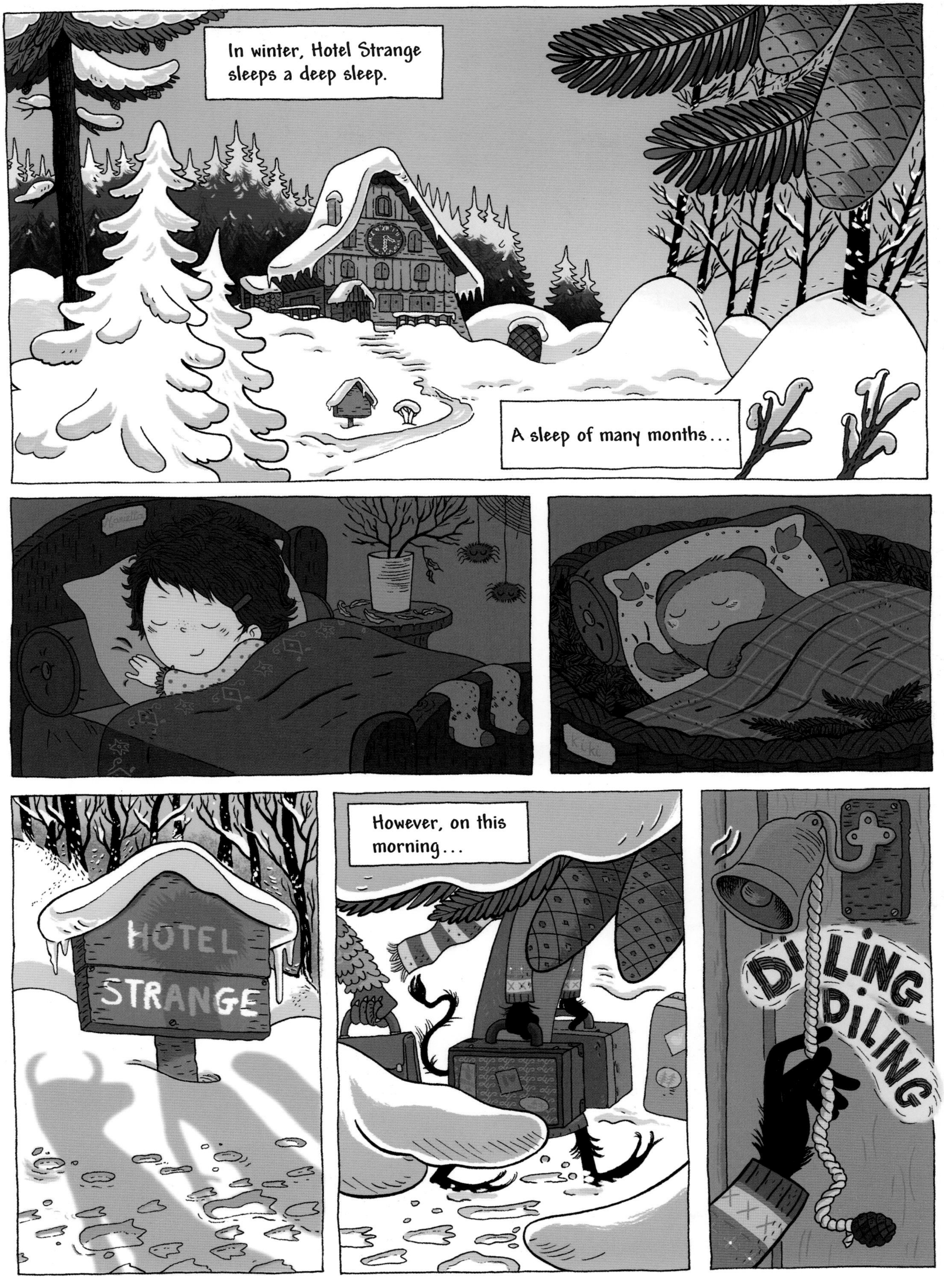
In winter, Hotel Strange sleeps a deep sleep.
A sleep of many months...
HOTEL STRANGE
However, on this morning...
DILING DILING

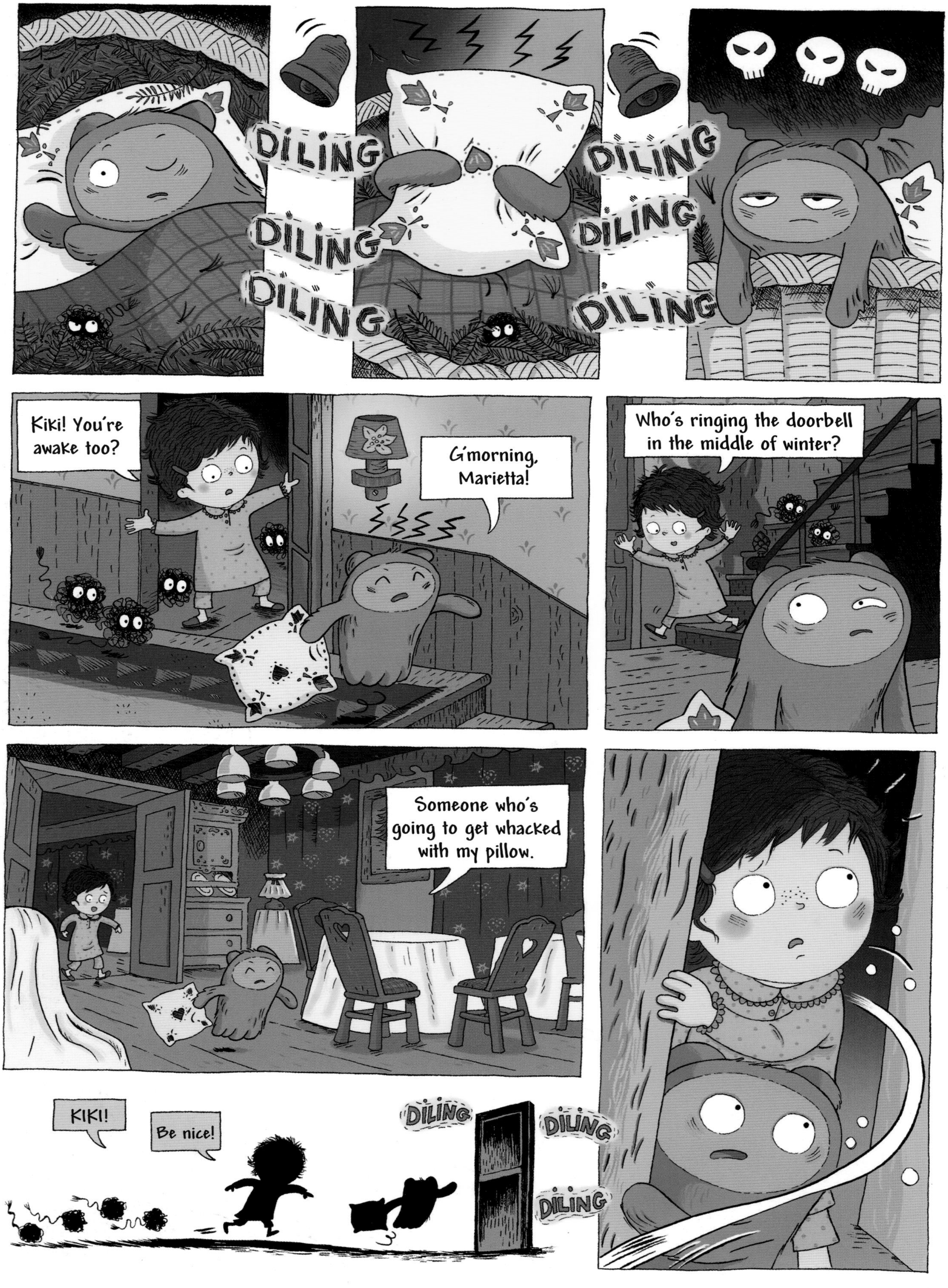
DILING
DILING
DILING
DILING
DILING
DILING
Kiki! You're awake too?
G'morning, Marietta!
Who's ringing the doorbell in the middle of winter?
Someone who's going to get whacked with my pillow.
KIKI!
Be nice!
DILING
DILING
DILING

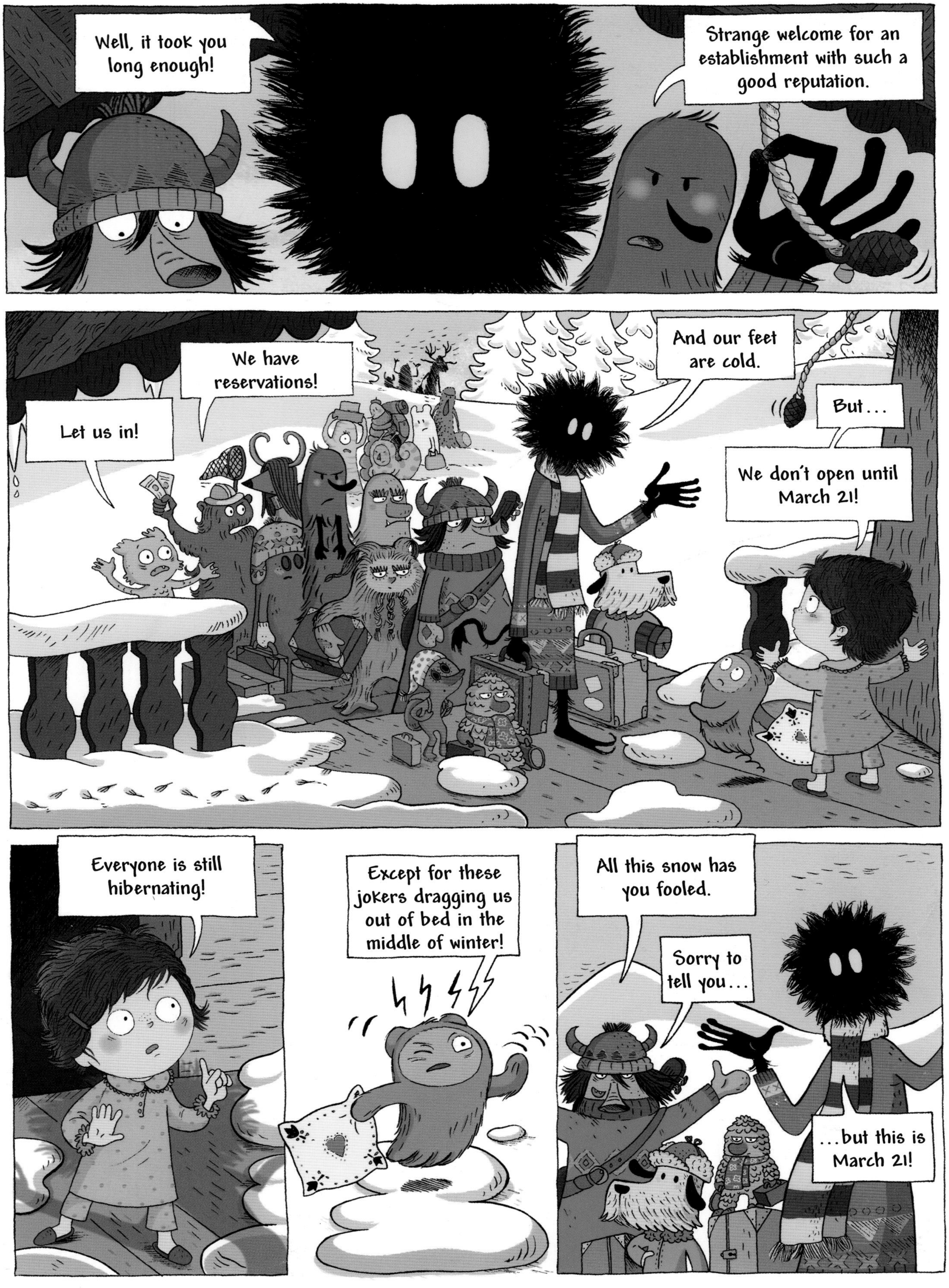

Well, it took you long enough!
Strange welcome for an establishment with such a good reputation.
Let us in!
We have reservations!
And our feet are cold.
But...
We don't open until March 21!
Everyone is still hibernating!
Except for these jokers dragging us out of bed in the middle of winter!
All this snow has you fooled.
Sorry to tell you...
...but this is March 21!

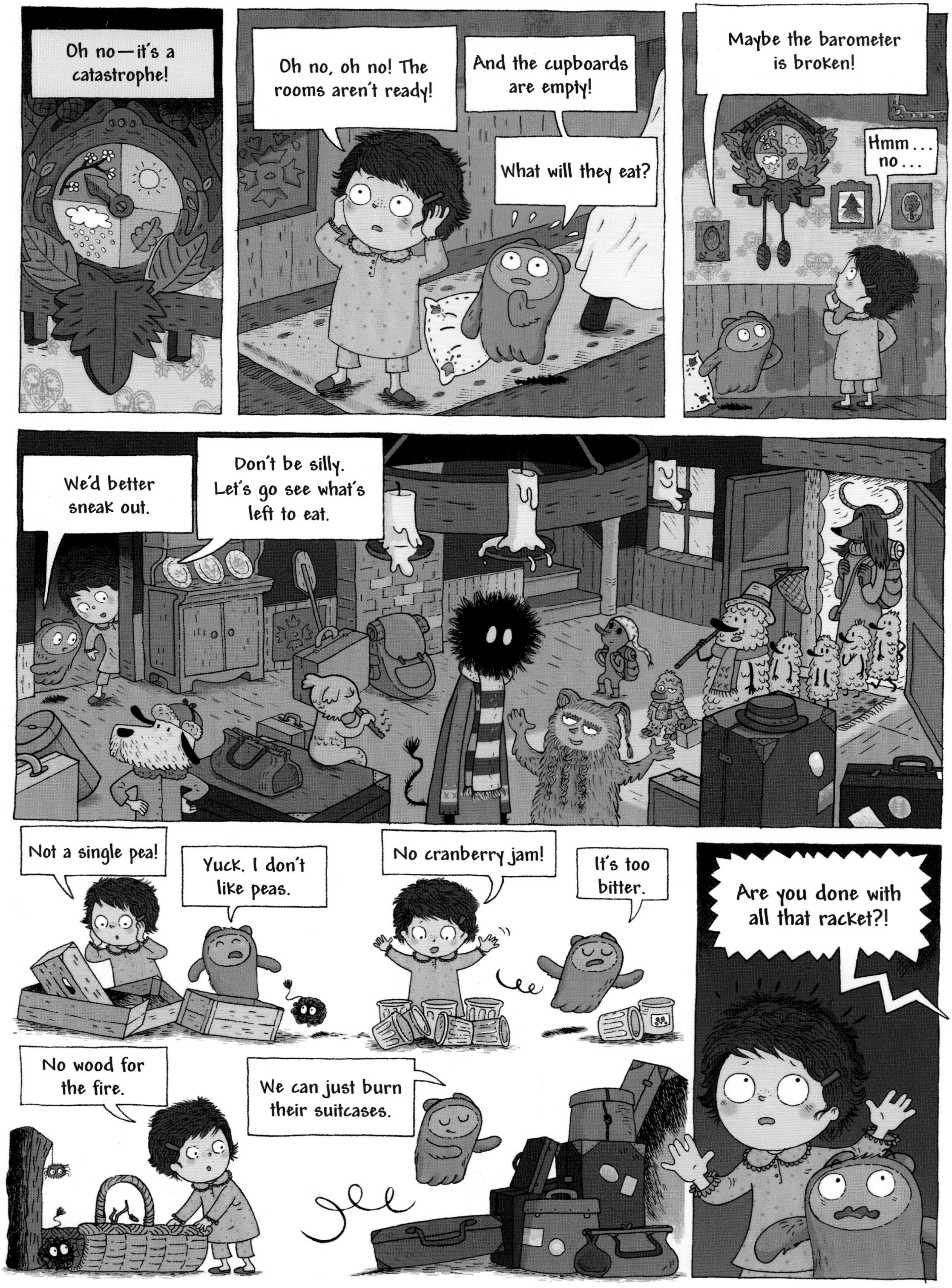

Oh no—it's a catastrophe!
Oh no, oh no! The rooms aren't ready!
And the cupboards are empty!
What will they eat?
Maybe the barometer is broken!
Hmm... no...
We'd better sneak out.
Don't be silly. Let's go see what's left to eat.
Not a single pea!
Yuck. I don't like peas.
No cranberry jam!
It's too bitter.
No wood for the fire.
We can just burn their suitcases.
Are you done with all that racket?!

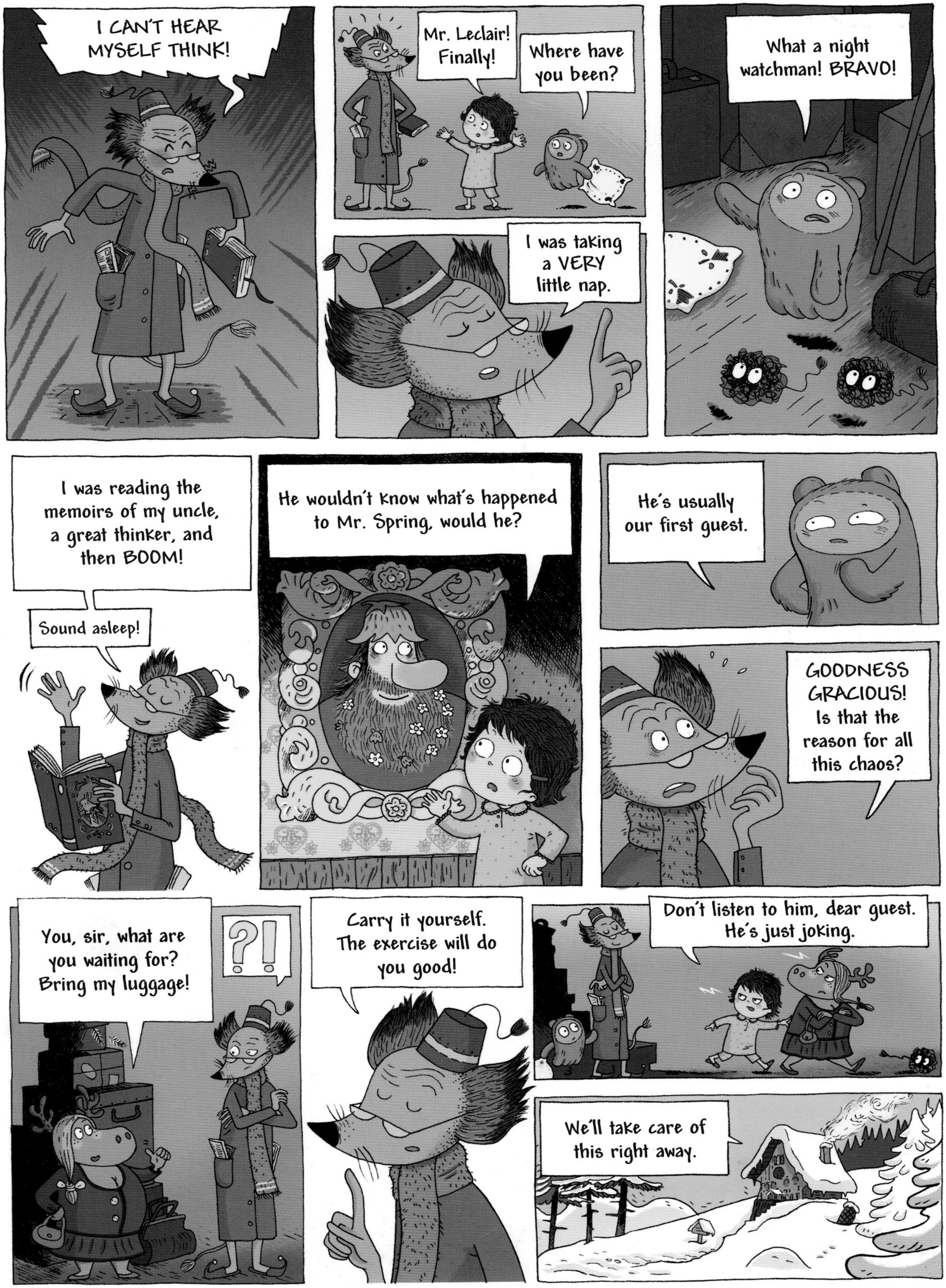
I CAN'T HEAR MYSELF THINK!
Mr. Leclair! Finally!
Where have you been?
I was taking a VERY little nap.
What a night watchman! BRAVO!
I was reading the memoirs of my uncle, a great thinker, and then BOOM!
Sound asleep!
He wouldn't know what's happened to Mr. Spring, would he?
He's usually our first guest.
GOODNESS GRACIOUS! Is that the reason for all this chaos?
You, sir, what are you waiting for? Bring my luggage!
?!
Carry it yourself. The exercise will do you good!
Don't listen to him, dear guest. He's just joking.
We'll take care of this right away.

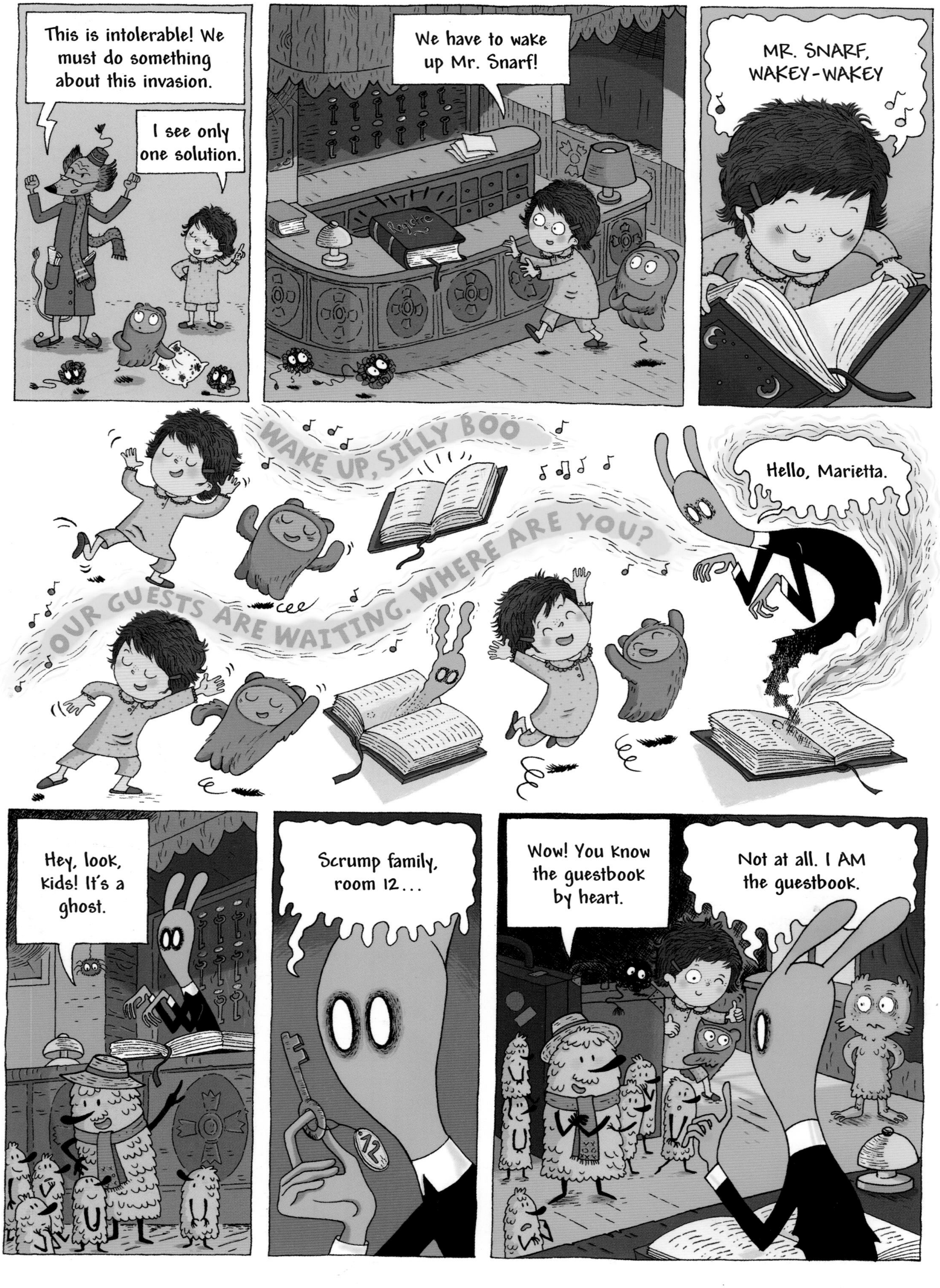
This is intolerable! We must do something about this invasion.
I see only one solution.
We have to wake up Mr. Snarf!
MR. SNARF, WAKEY-WAKEY
WAKE UP, SILLY BOO
OUR GUESTS ARE WAITING. WHERE ARE YOU?
Hello, Marietta.
Hey, look, kids! It's a ghost.
Scrump family, room 12...
Wow! You know the guestbook by heart.
Not at all. I AM the guestbook.

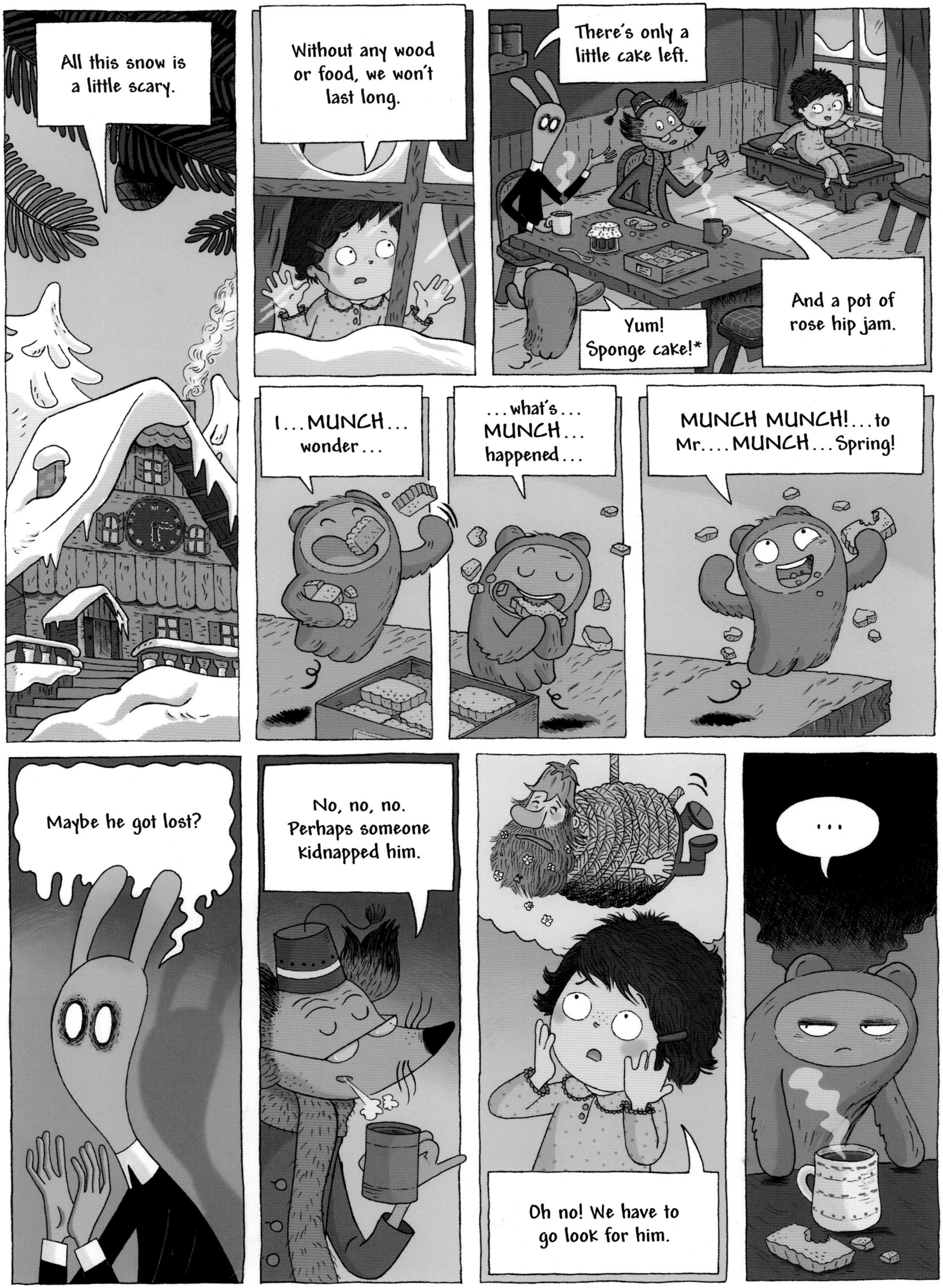

All this snow is a little scary.
Without any wood or food, we won't last long.
There's only a little cake left.
Yum! Sponge cake!*
And a pot of rose hip jam.
I... MUNCH... wonder...
...what's... MUNCH... happened...
MUNCH MUNCH!...to Mr.... MUNCH... Spring!
Maybe he got lost?
No, no, no. Perhaps someone kidnapped him.
Oh no! We have to go look for him.
...

*See the SPONGE CAKE recipe at the end of the book!

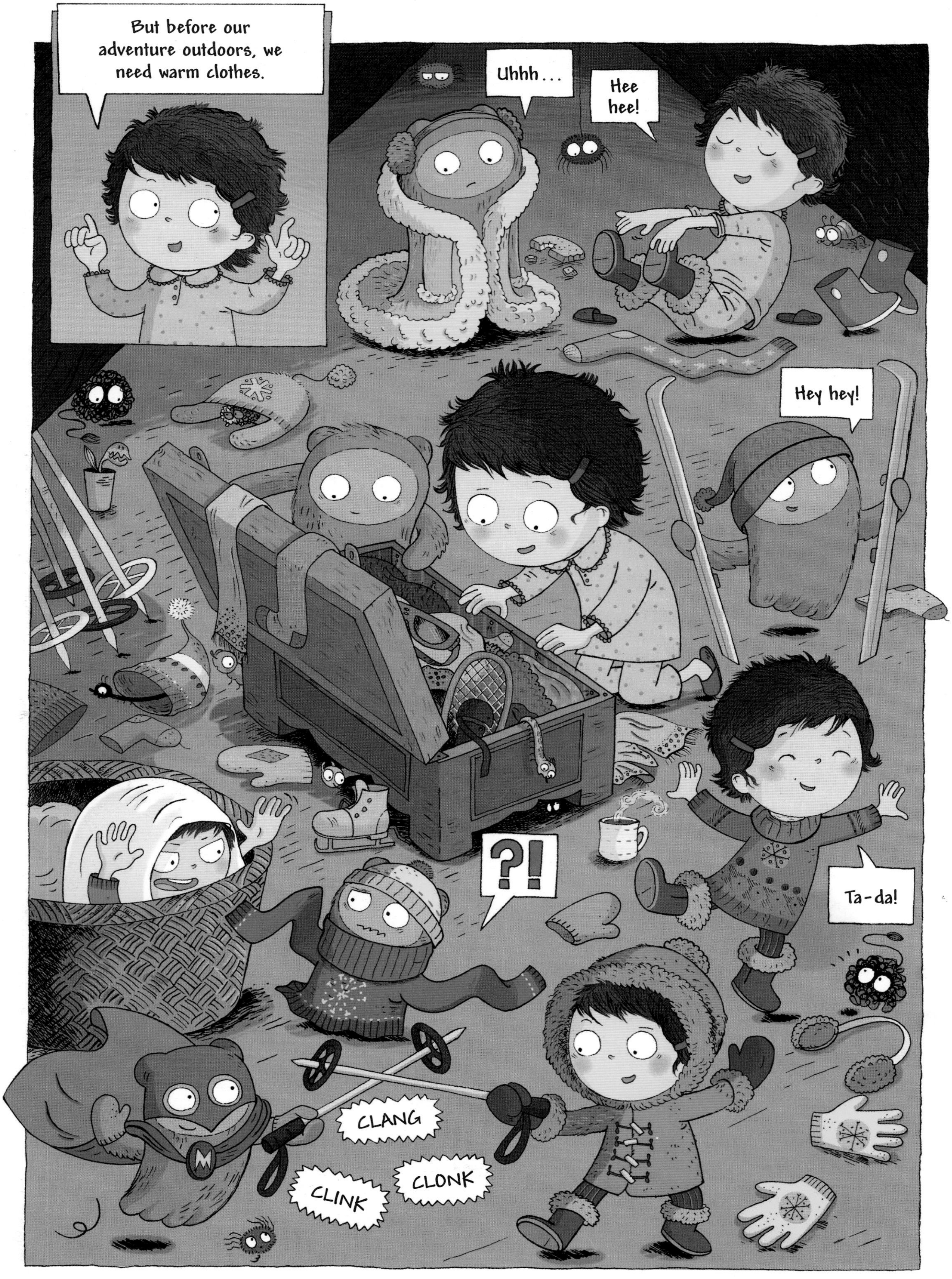
But before our adventure outdoors, we need warm clothes.
Uhhh...
Hee hee!
Hey hey!
?!
Ta-da!
CLANG
CLONK
CLINK

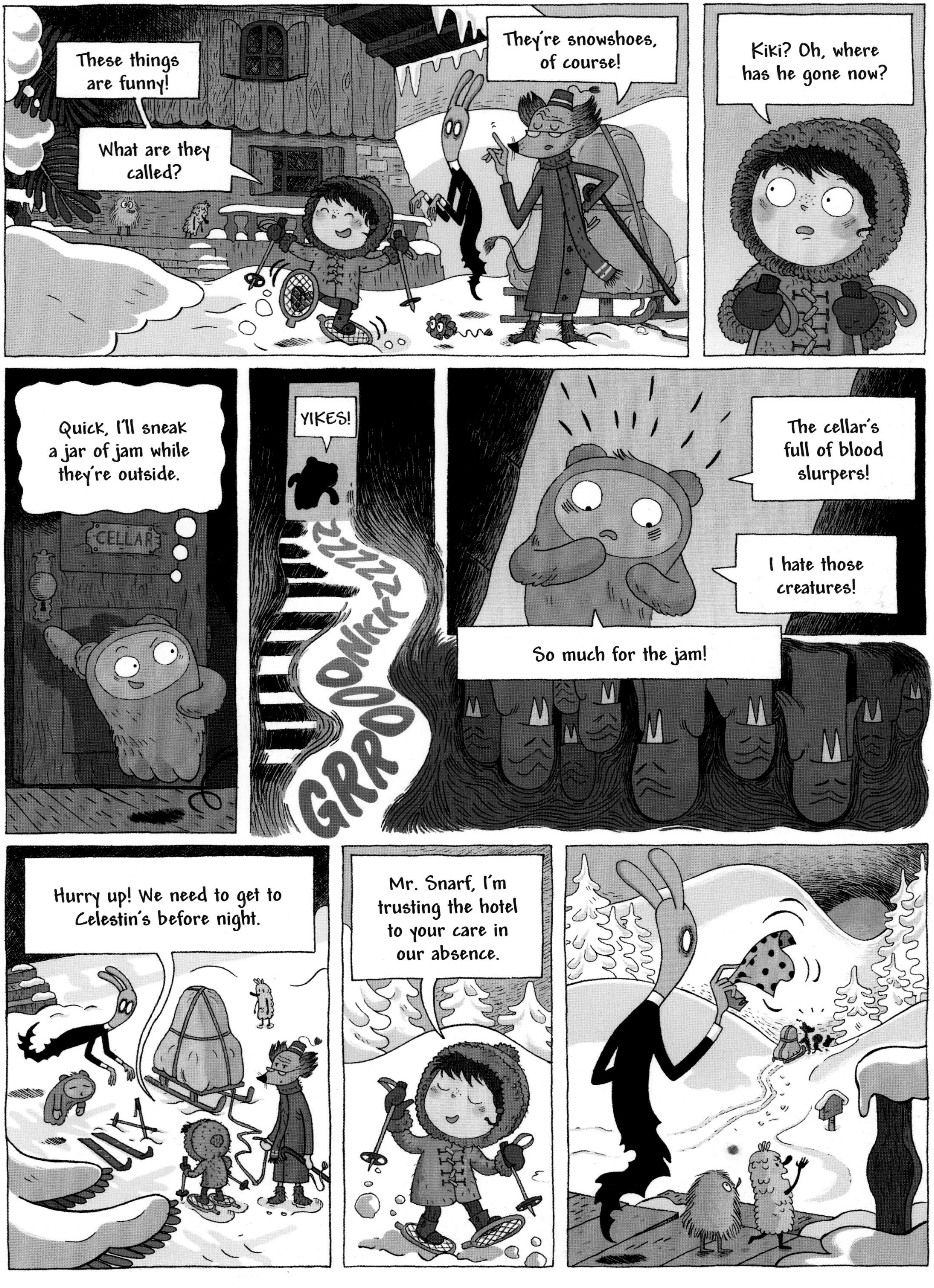
These things are funny!
What are they called?
They're snowshoes, of course!
Kiki? Oh, where has he gone now?
Quick, I'll sneak a jar of jam while they're outside.
CELLAR
YIKES!
GRROOOONKK-ZZZZZ
The cellar's full of blood slurpers!
I hate those creatures!
So much for the jam!
Hurry up! We need to get to Celestin's before night.
Mr. Snarf, I'm trusting the hotel to your care in our absence.

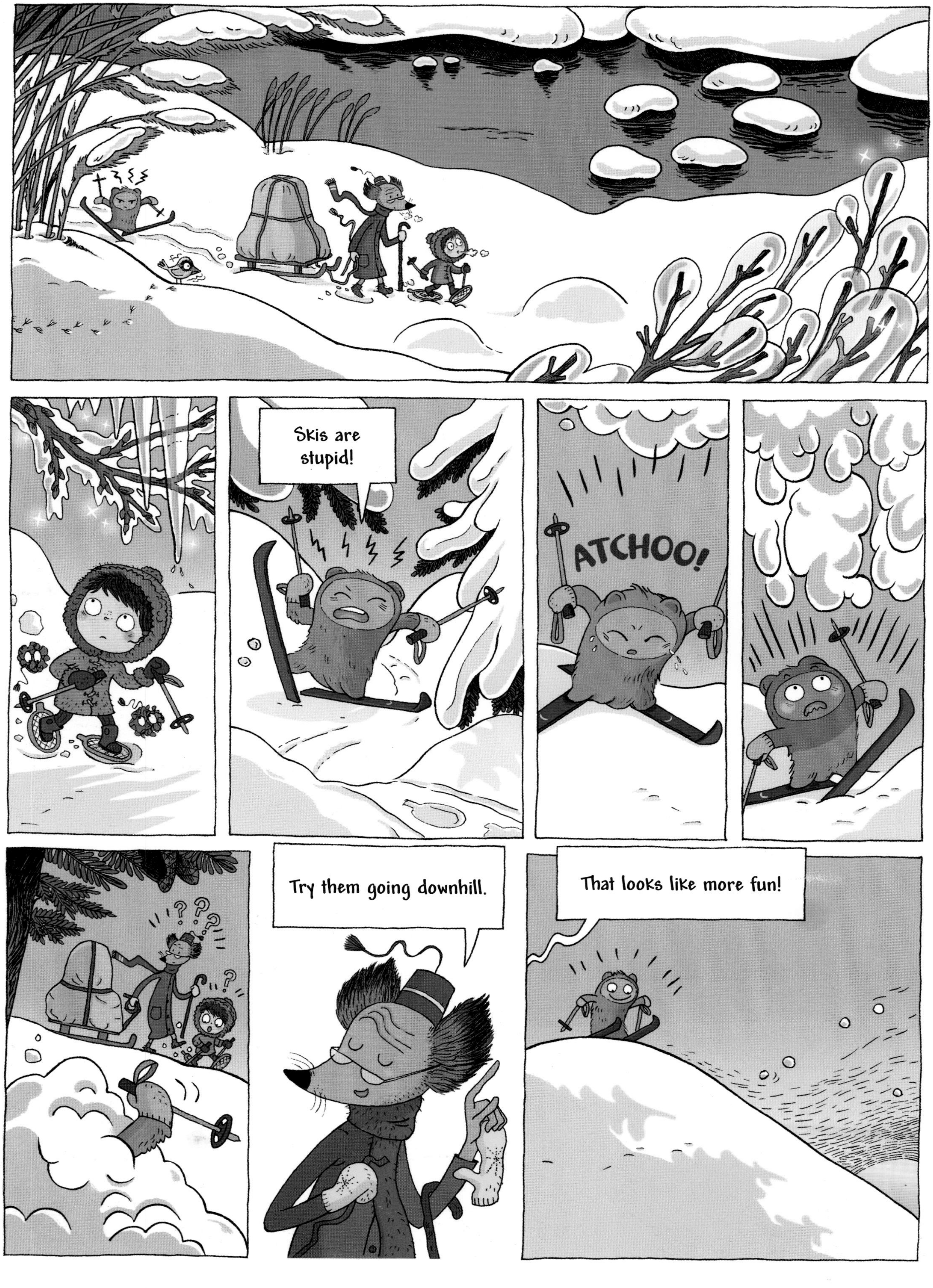
Skis are stupid!
ATCHOO!
Try them going downhill.
That looks like more fun!

WHOA

YEOW YEOW YEOW

YEEOW

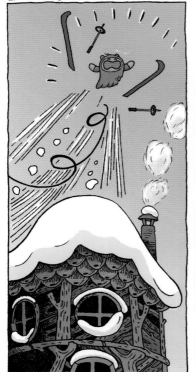

Hi there, Kiki.

You're just in time!

I could use a hand.

13

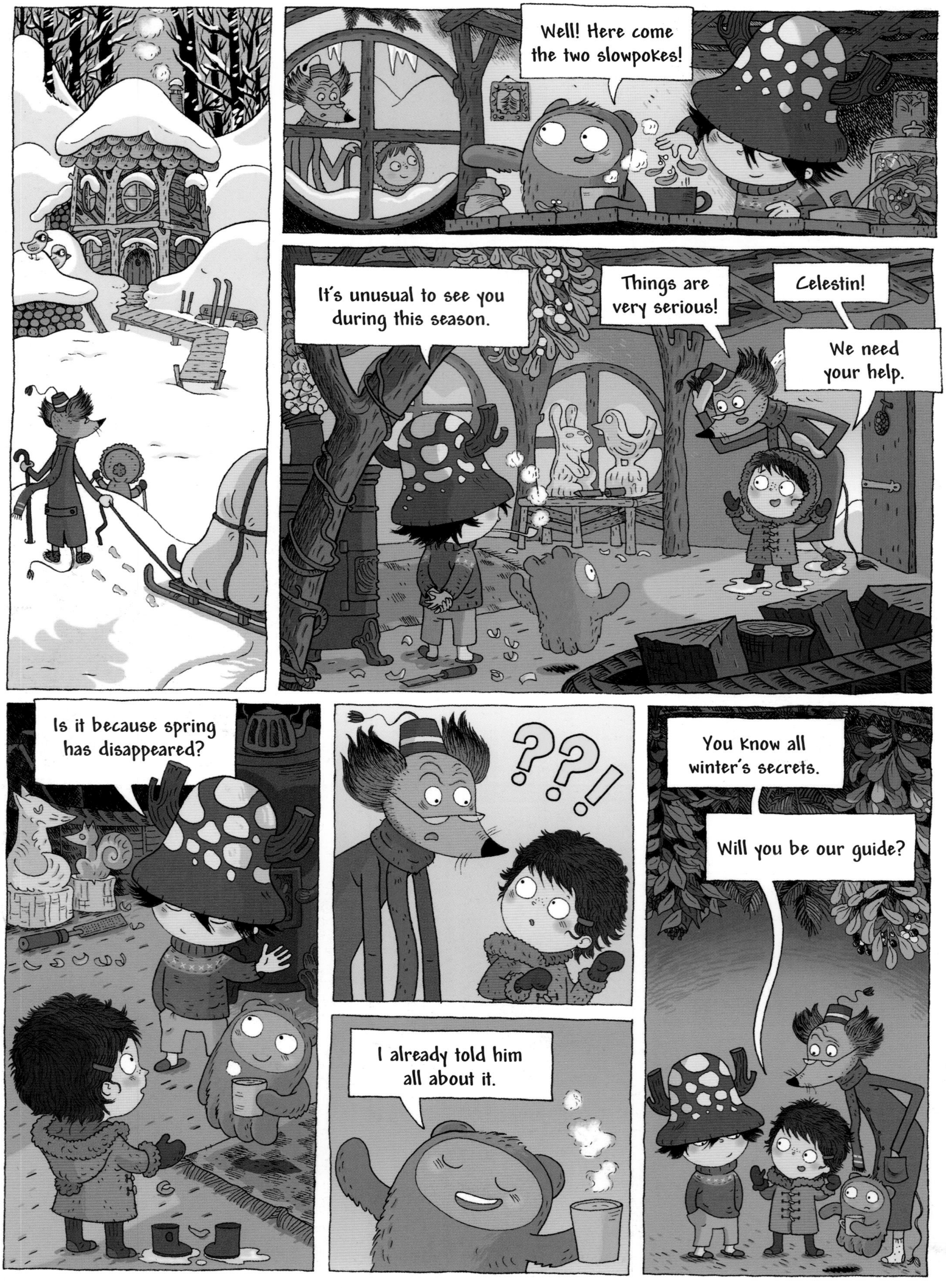

Well! Here come the two slowpokes!
It's unusual to see you during this season.
Things are very serious!
Celestin!
We need your help.
Is it because spring has disappeared?
??!
I already told him all about it.
You know all winter's secrets.
Will you be our guide?

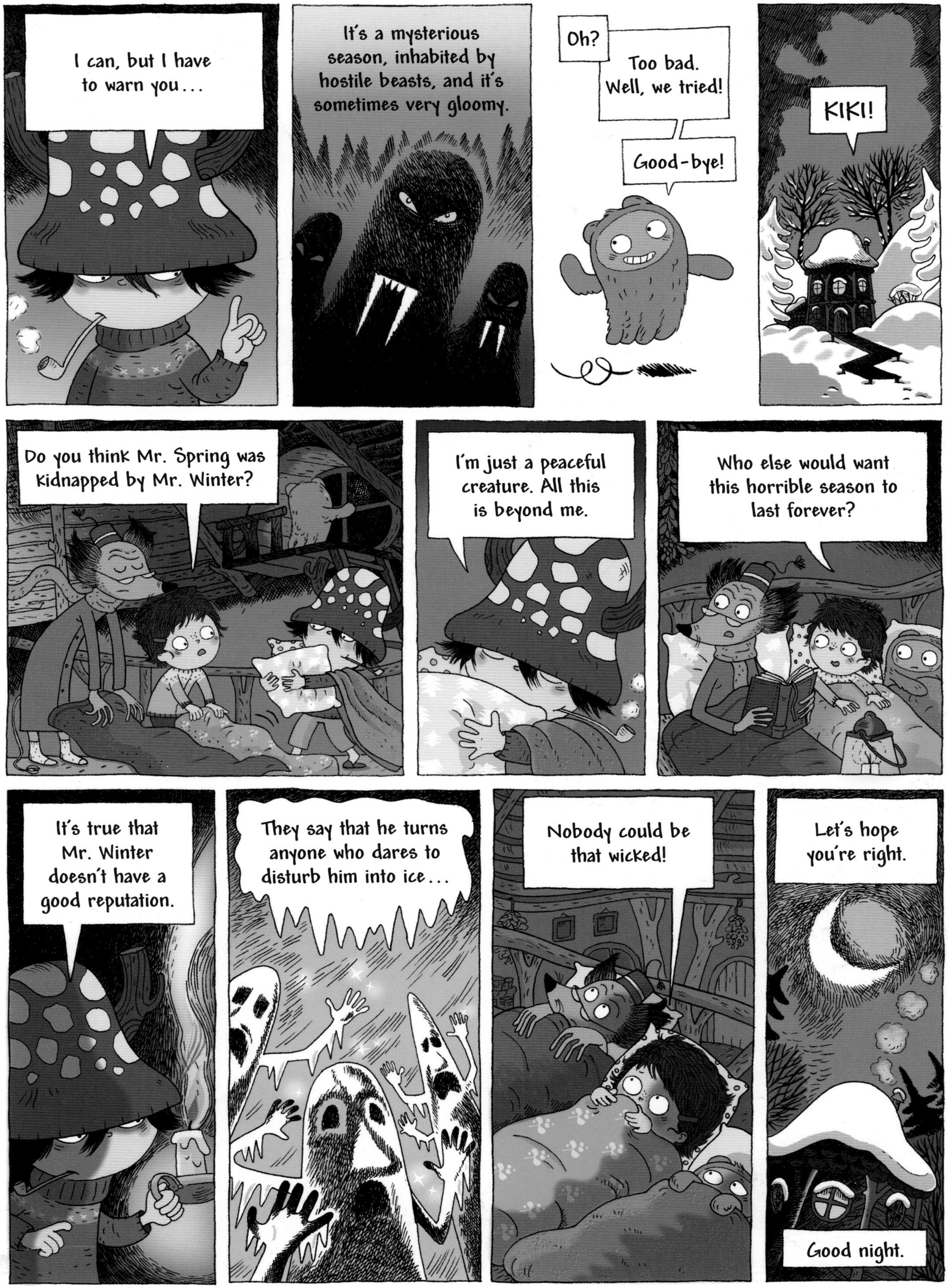
I can, but I have to warn you . . .
It's a mysterious season, inhabited by hostile beasts, and it's sometimes very gloomy.
Oh?
Too bad. Well, we tried!
Good-bye!
KIKI!
Do you think Mr. Spring was kidnapped by Mr. Winter?
I'm just a peaceful creature. All this is beyond me.
Who else would want this horrible season to last forever?
It's true that Mr. Winter doesn't have a good reputation.
They say that he turns anyone who dares to disturb him into ice . . .
Nobody could be that wicked!
Let's hope you're right.
Good night.

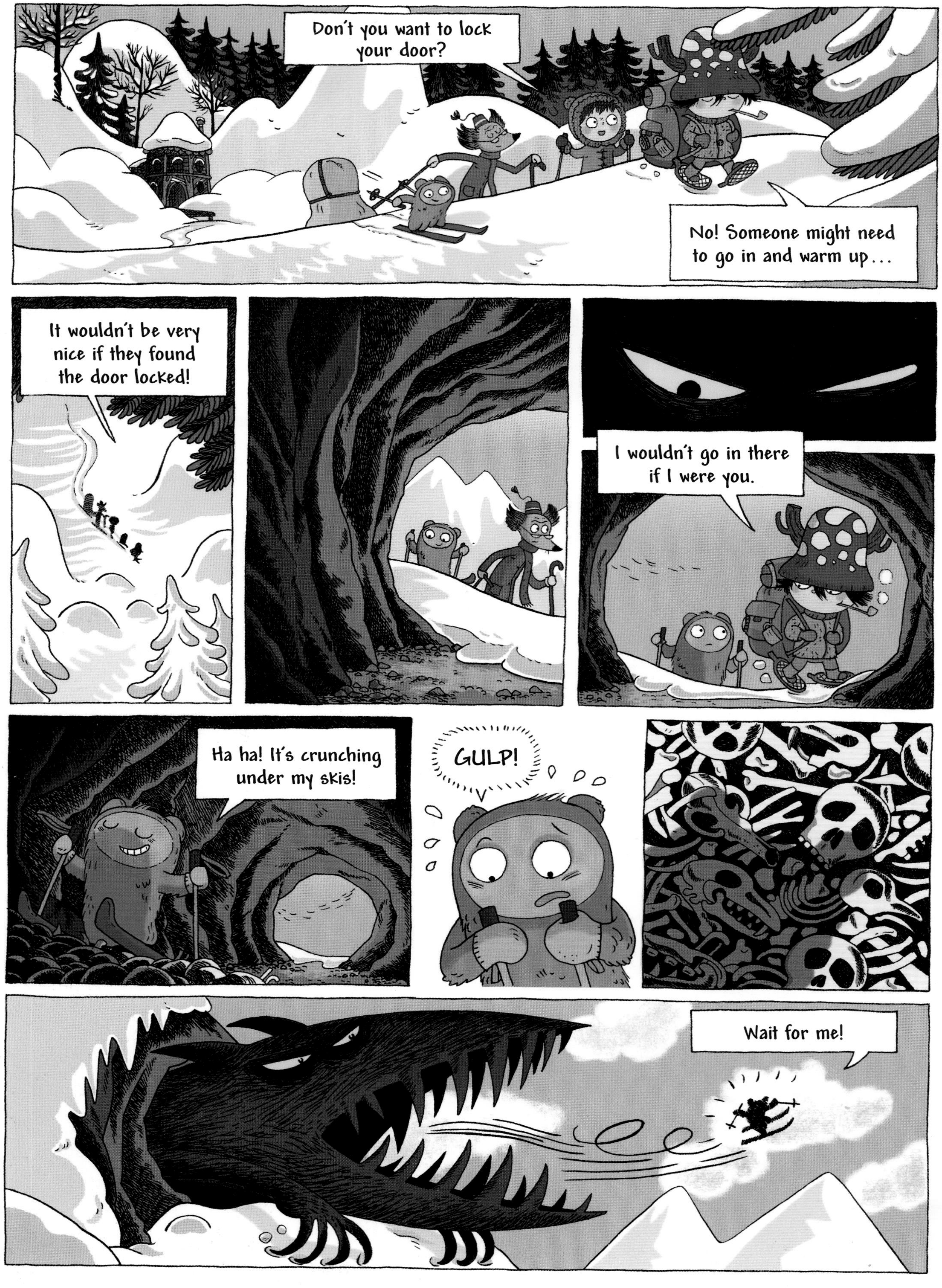
Don't you want to lock your door?
No! Someone might need to go in and warm up...
It wouldn't be very nice if they found the door locked!
I wouldn't go in there if I were you.
Ha ha! It's crunching under my skis!
GULP!
Wait for me!

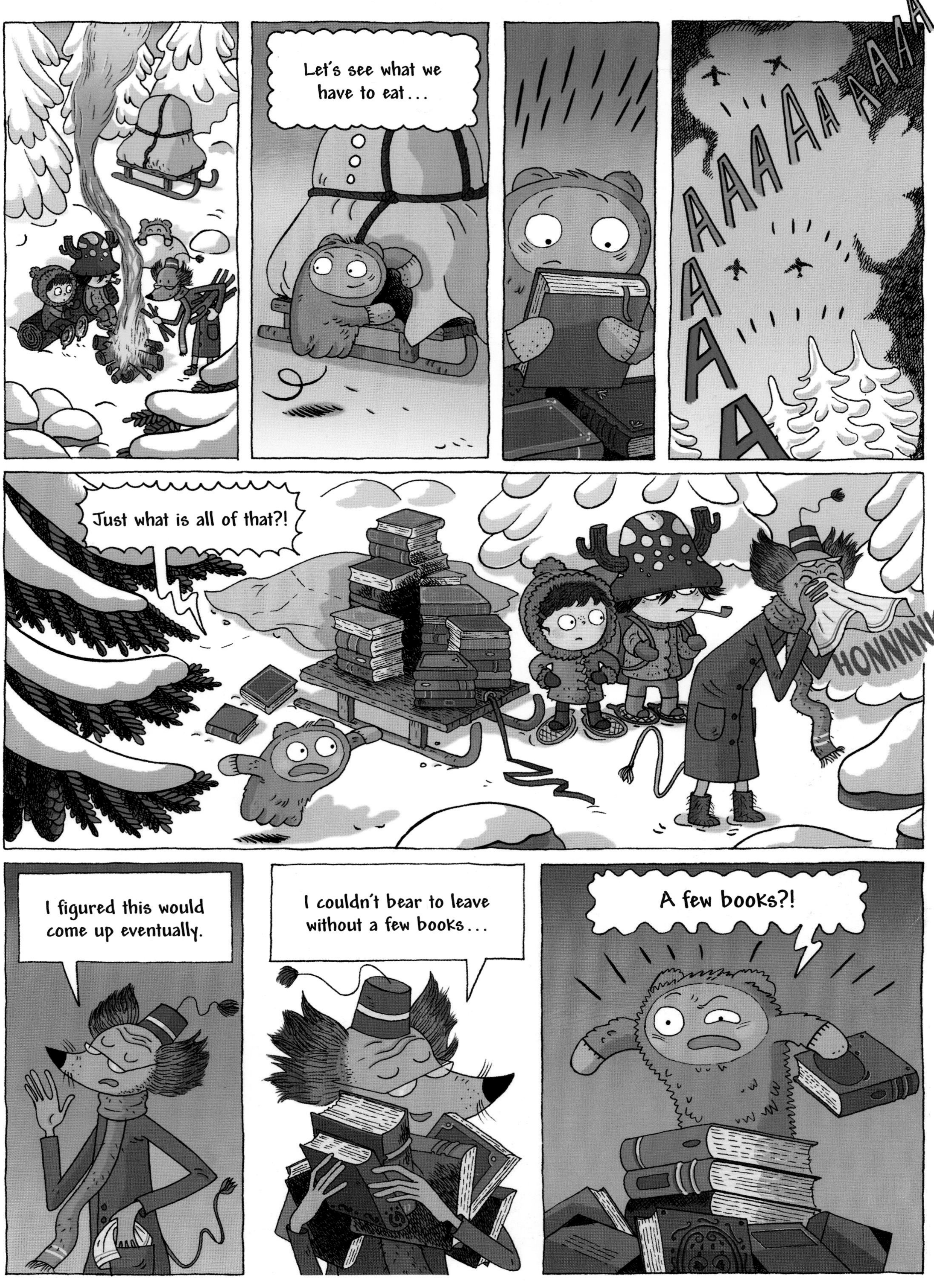

Let's see what we have to eat...
AAAAAAAAAAAAAAAA
Just what is all of that?!
HONNNNK!
I figured this would come up eventually.
I couldn't bear to leave without a few books...
A few books?!

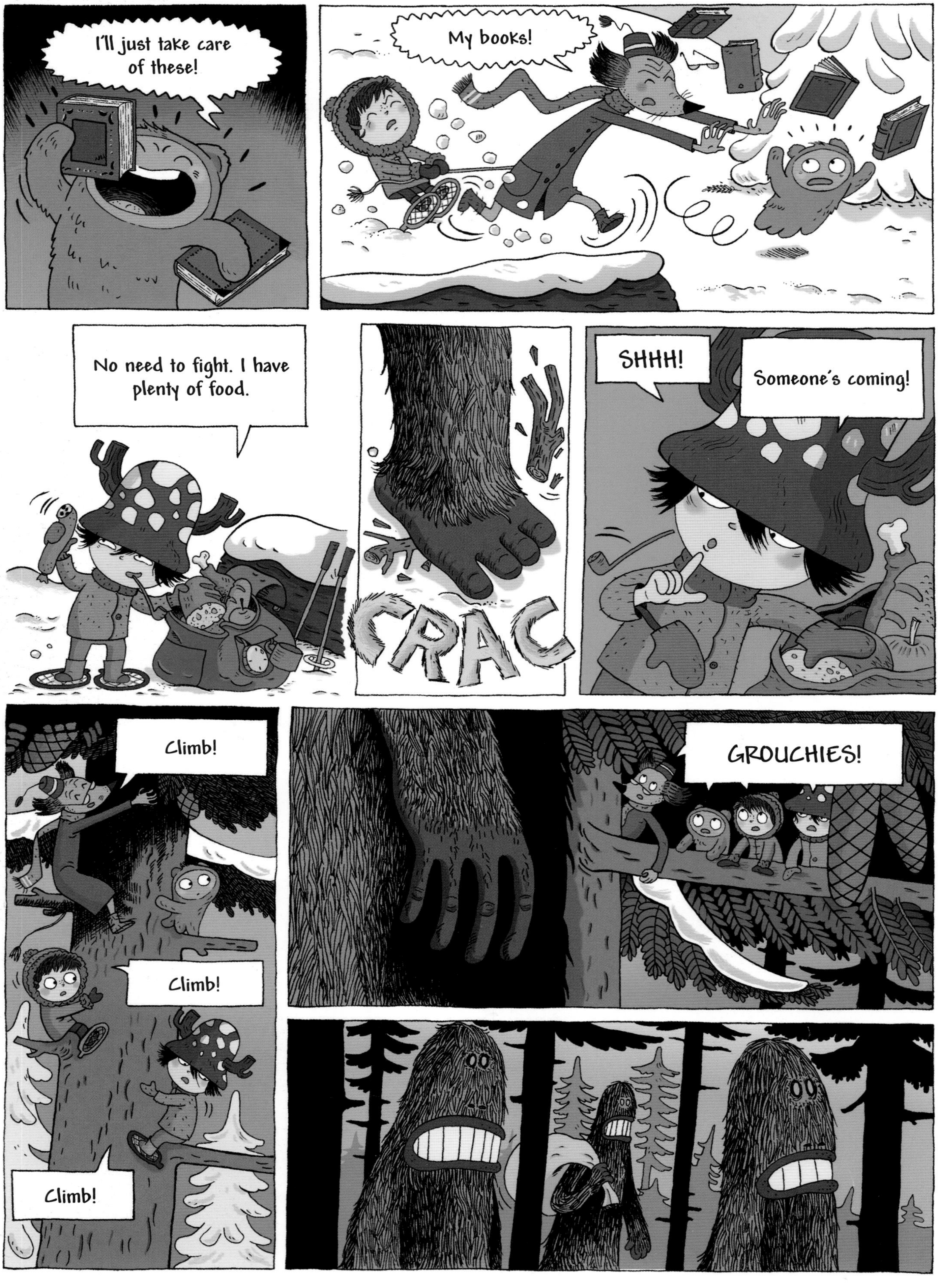
I'll just take care of these!
My books!
No need to fight. I have plenty of food.
CRAC
SHHH!
Someone's coming!
Climb!
Climb!
Climb!
GROUCHIES!

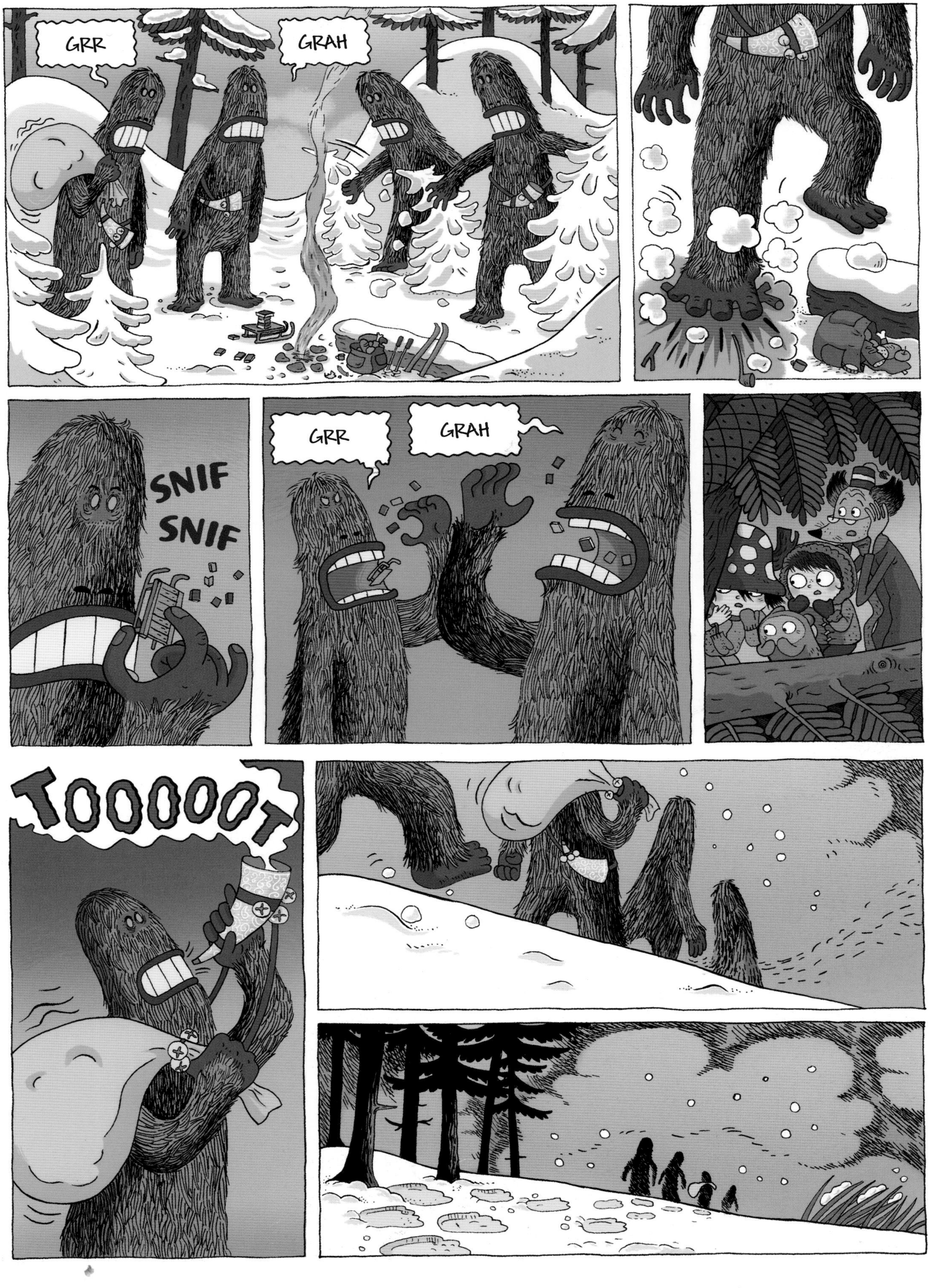
GRR
GRAH
SNIF
SNIF
GRR
GRAH
TOOOOOT

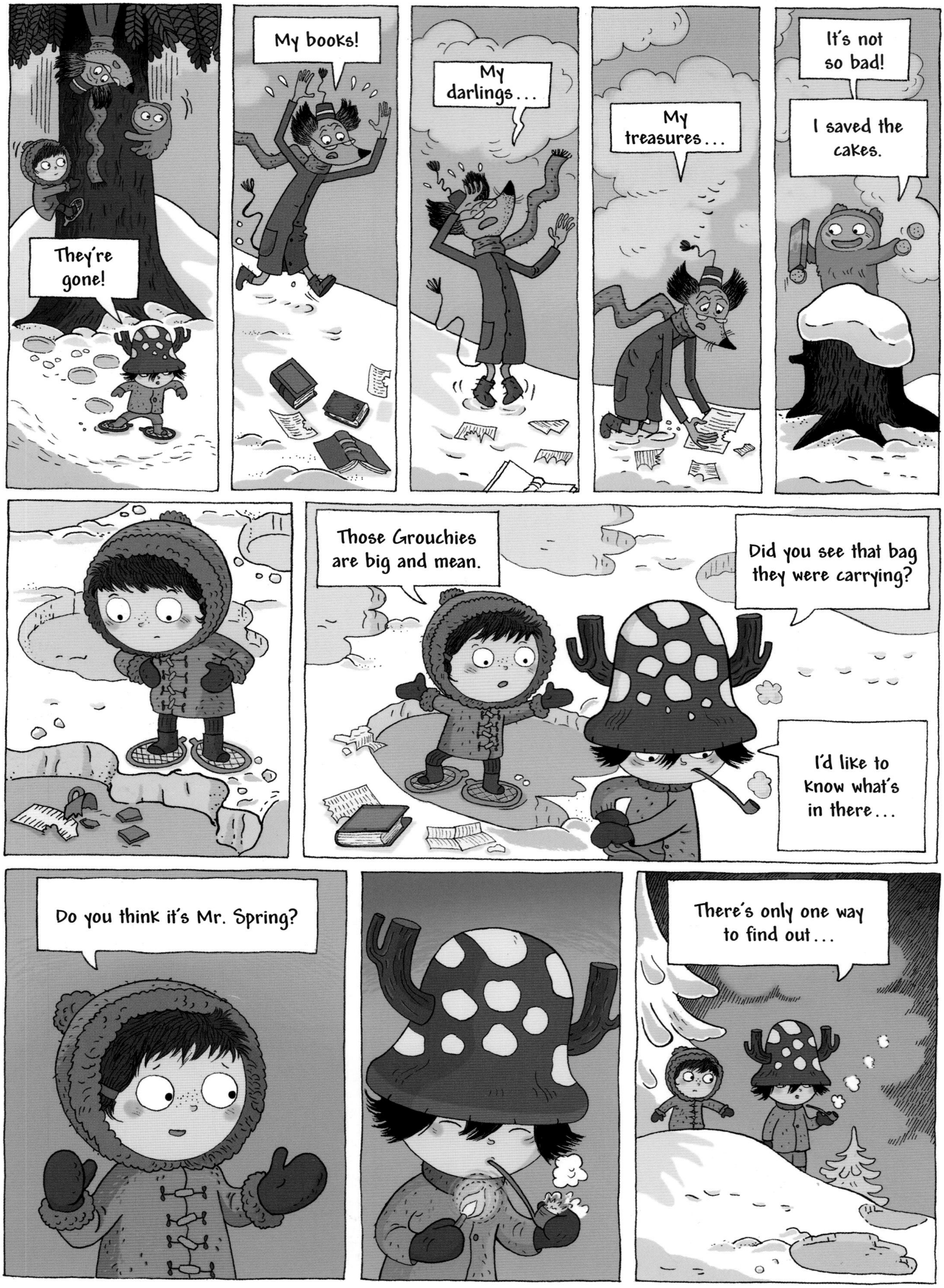

They're gone!
My books!
My darlings...
My treasures...
It's not so bad!
I saved the cakes.
Those Grouchies are big and mean.
Did you see that bag they were carrying?
I'd like to know what's in there...
Do you think it's Mr. Spring?
There's only one way to find out...

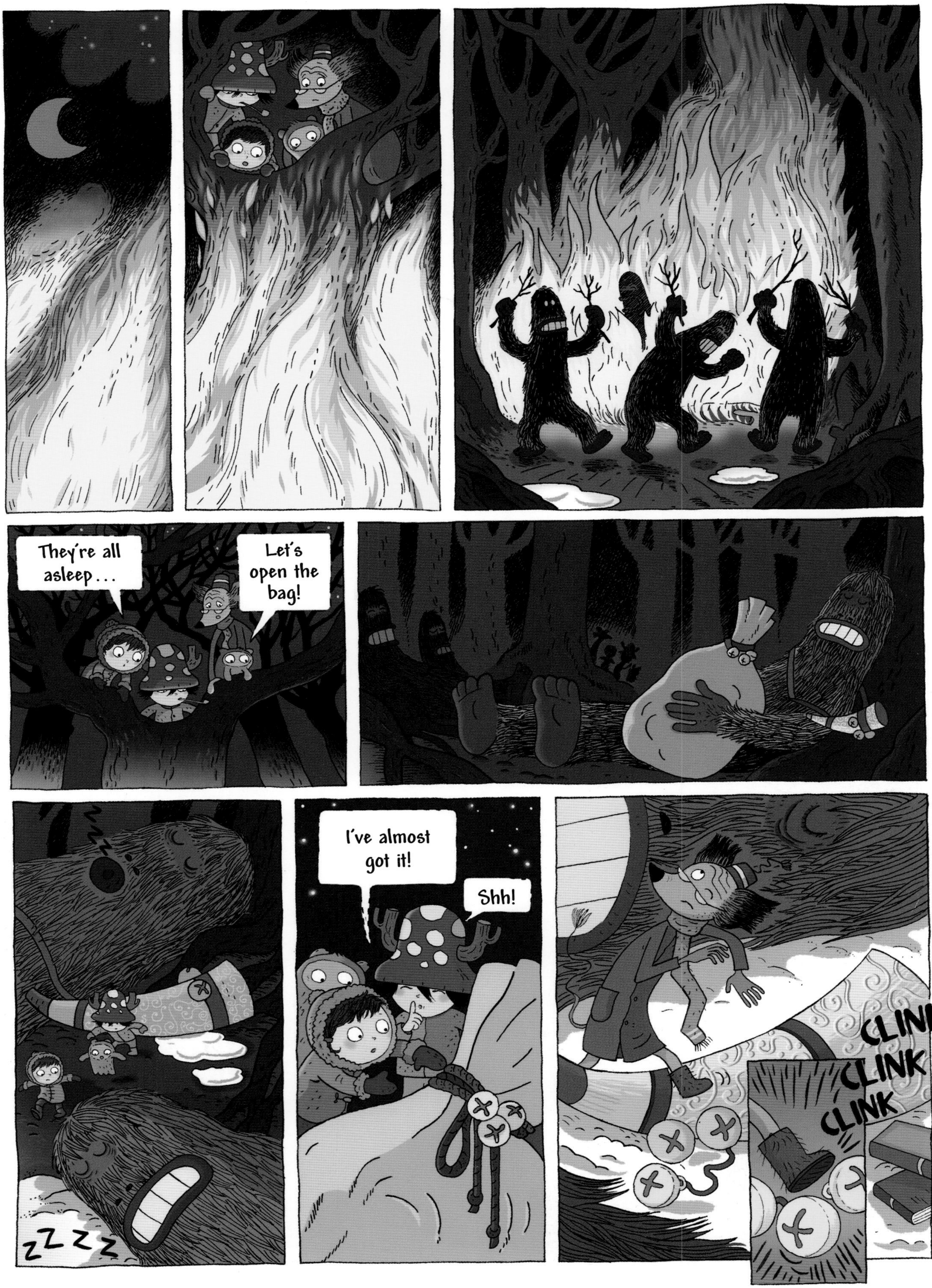

They're all asleep...
Let's open the bag!
ZZZZ
I've almost got it!
Shh!
CLINK
CLINK
CLINK

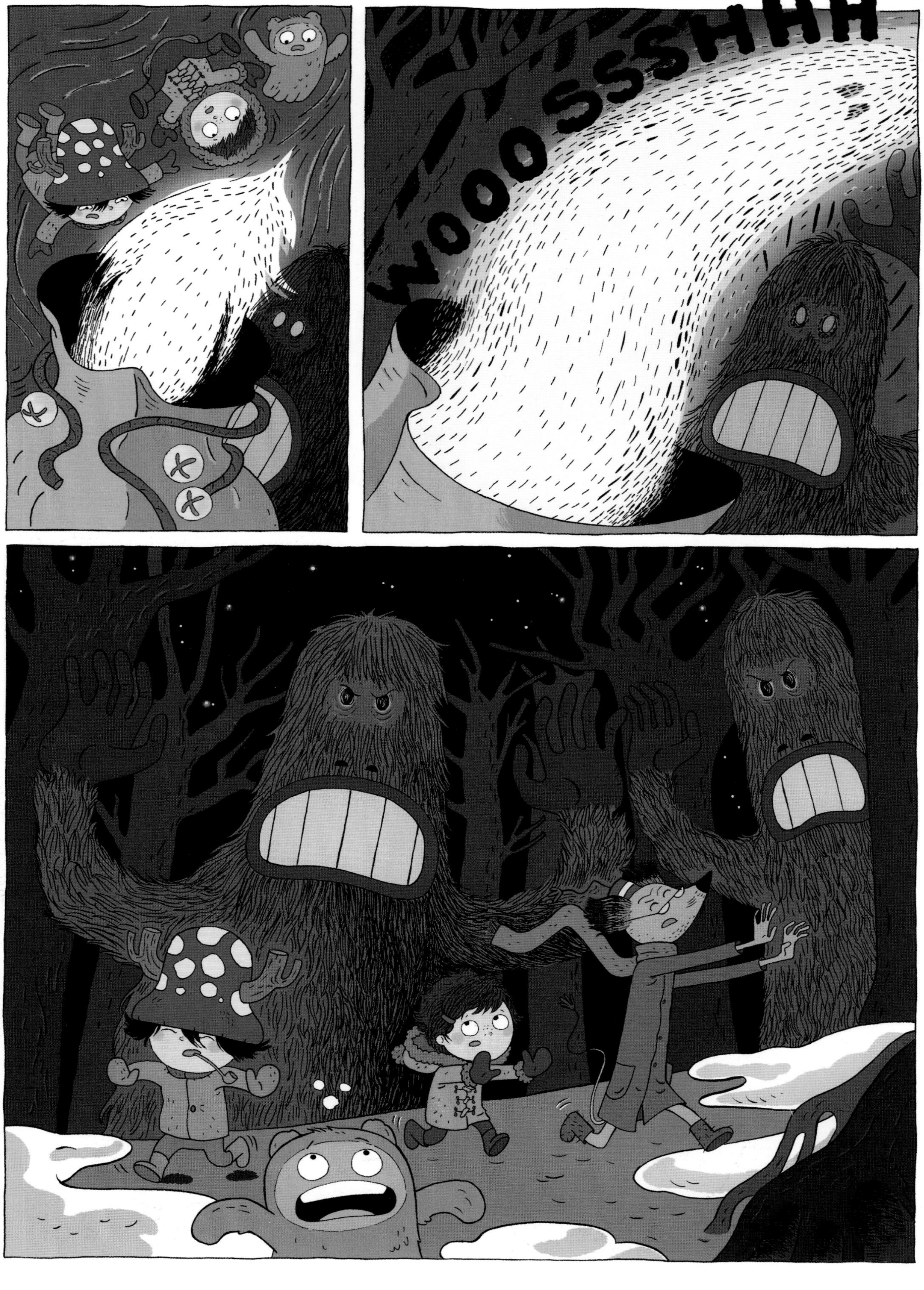
WOOOSSSHHH

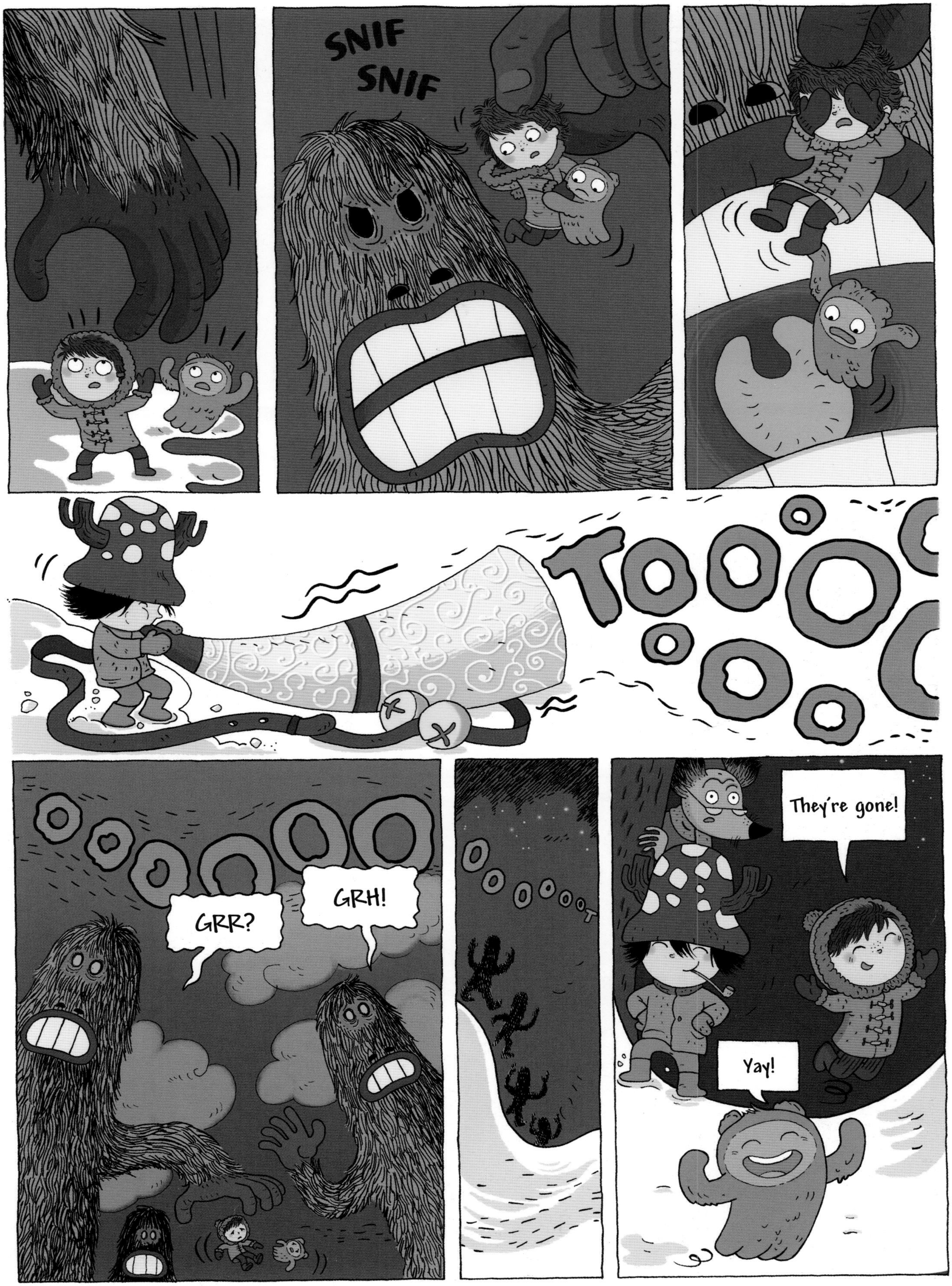

SNIF
SNIF
TOOOO
OOOOOO
GRR?
GRH!
OOOOOOT
They're gone!
Yay!

I've never seen creatures like that!

They're always angry.

And hungry.

Luckily, we got all our things back.

Did anyone see what was in the bag?

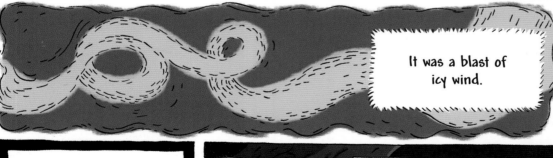

It was a blast of icy wind.

Yes, but...

Kiki, quiet down! And go to sleep.

I thought it would be Mr. Spring.

Too bad! We're going to Mr. Winter's house, and that's that.

The next morning...

Look at that.

Some night watchman he is.

Mr. Leclair! We have a long road to travel!

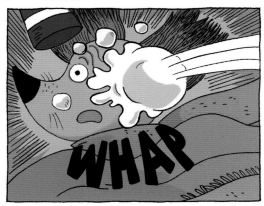

WHAP

That was fun.

Hurry up! Look at that fog.

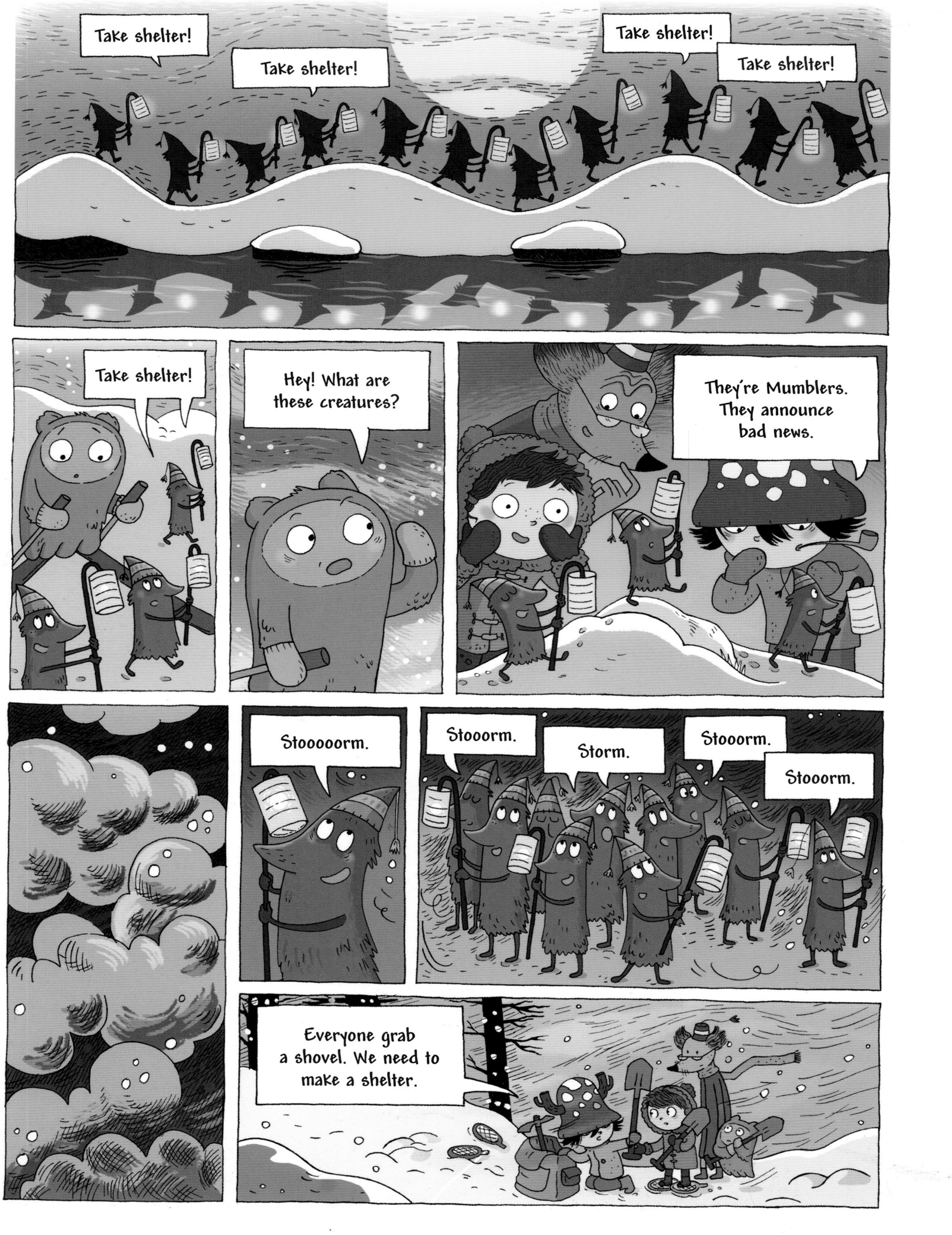
Take shelter!
Take shelter!
Take shelter!
Take shelter!
Take shelter!
Hey! What are these creatures?
They're Mumblers. They announce bad news.
Stoooooorm.
Stooorm.
Storm.
Stooorm.
Stooorm.
Everyone grab a shovel. We need to make a shelter.

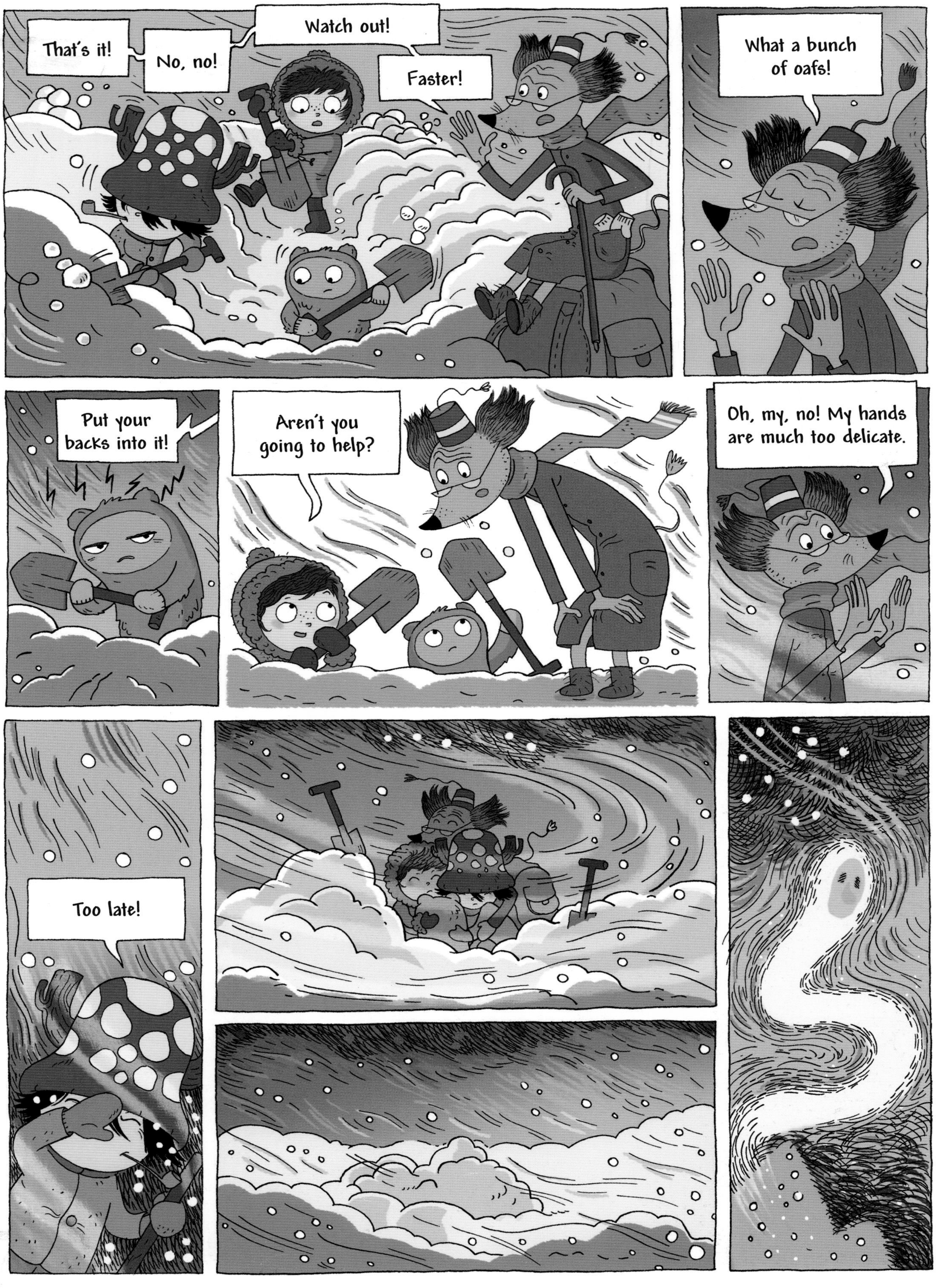

That's it!
No, no!
Watch out!
Faster!
What a bunch of oafs!
Put your backs into it!
Aren't you going to help?
Oh, my, no! My hands are much too delicate.
Too late!

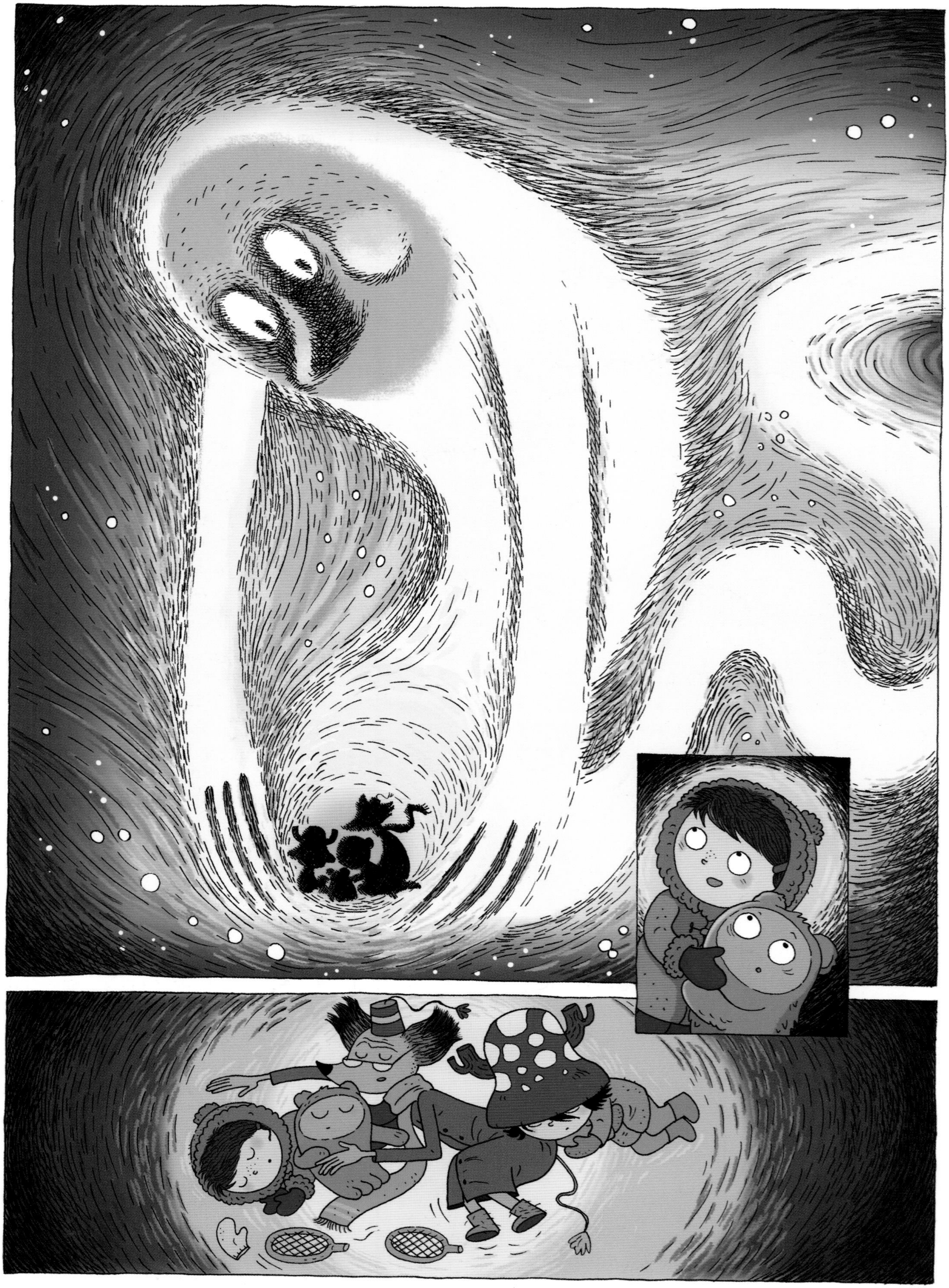

CRICK
CRACK

Wake up! The storm is over!

Did you see the strange creature that built our igloo?

That was a Smog, a fog-beast.

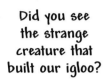

It left before we could say thank you.

I have a feeling that it was thanking us.

Why? We've never met!

Remember the bag the Grouchies had.

The Smog was their prisoner.

So we freed it?

Yes!

You see that smoke?

That's Mr. Winter's house.

29

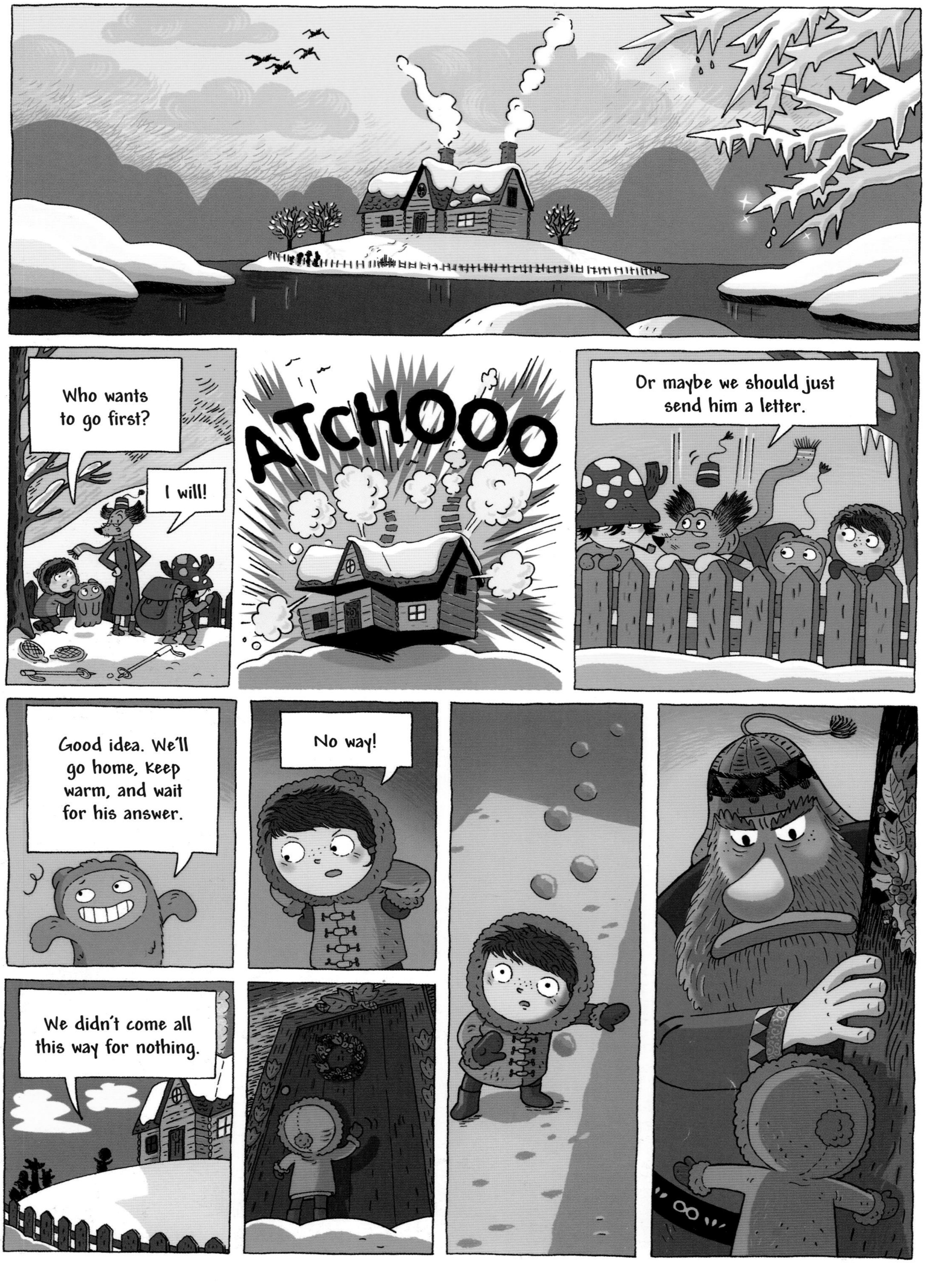
Who wants to go first?
I will!
ATCHOOO
Or maybe we should just send him a letter.
Good idea. We'll go home, keep warm, and wait for his answer.
No way!
We didn't come all this way for nothing.

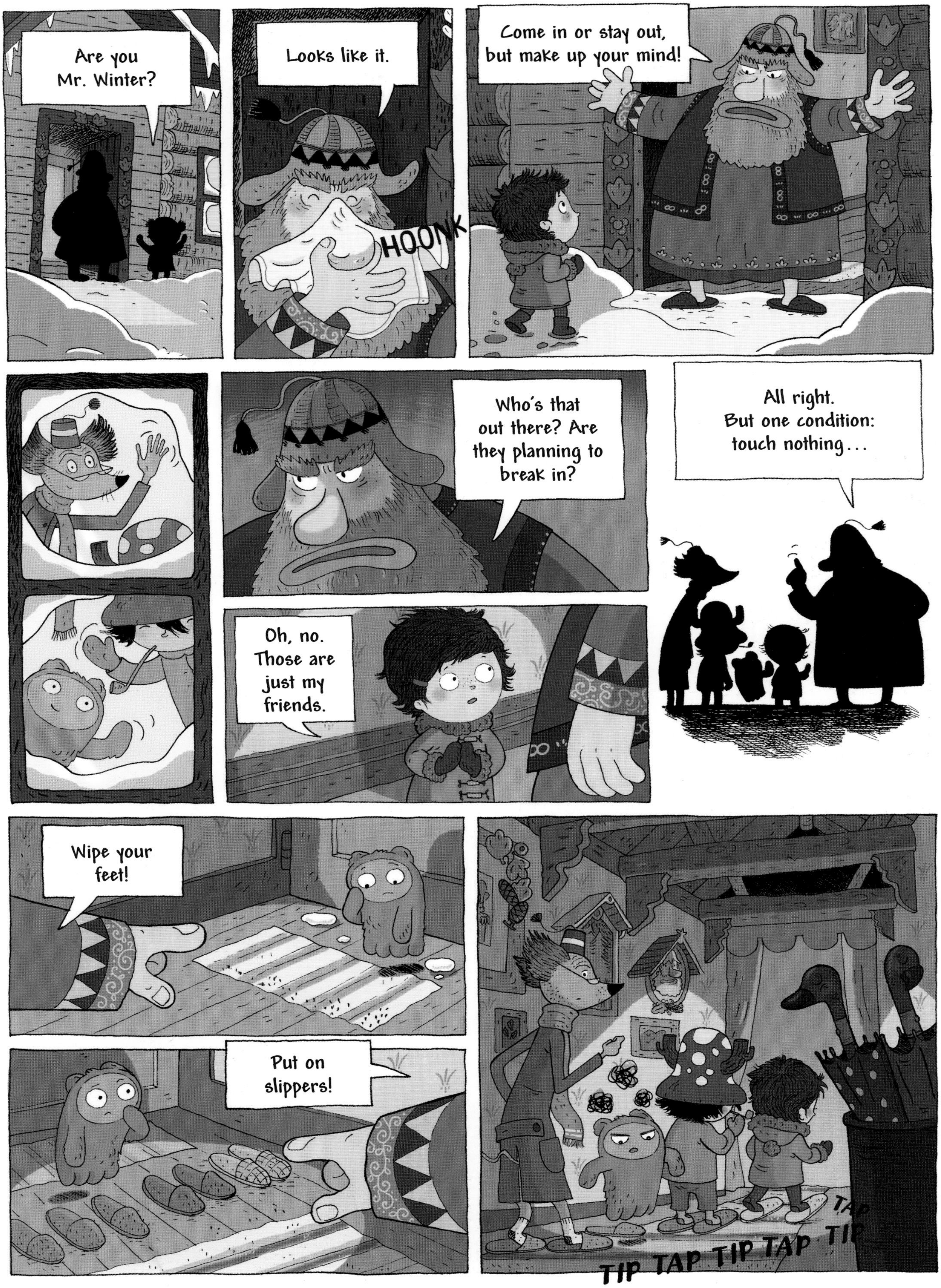
Are you Mr. Winter?
Looks like it.
HOONK
Come in or stay out, but make up your mind!
Who's that out there? Are they planning to break in?
Oh, no. Those are just my friends.
All right. But one condition: touch nothing...
Wipe your feet!
Put on slippers!
TIP TAP TIP TAP TIP TAP

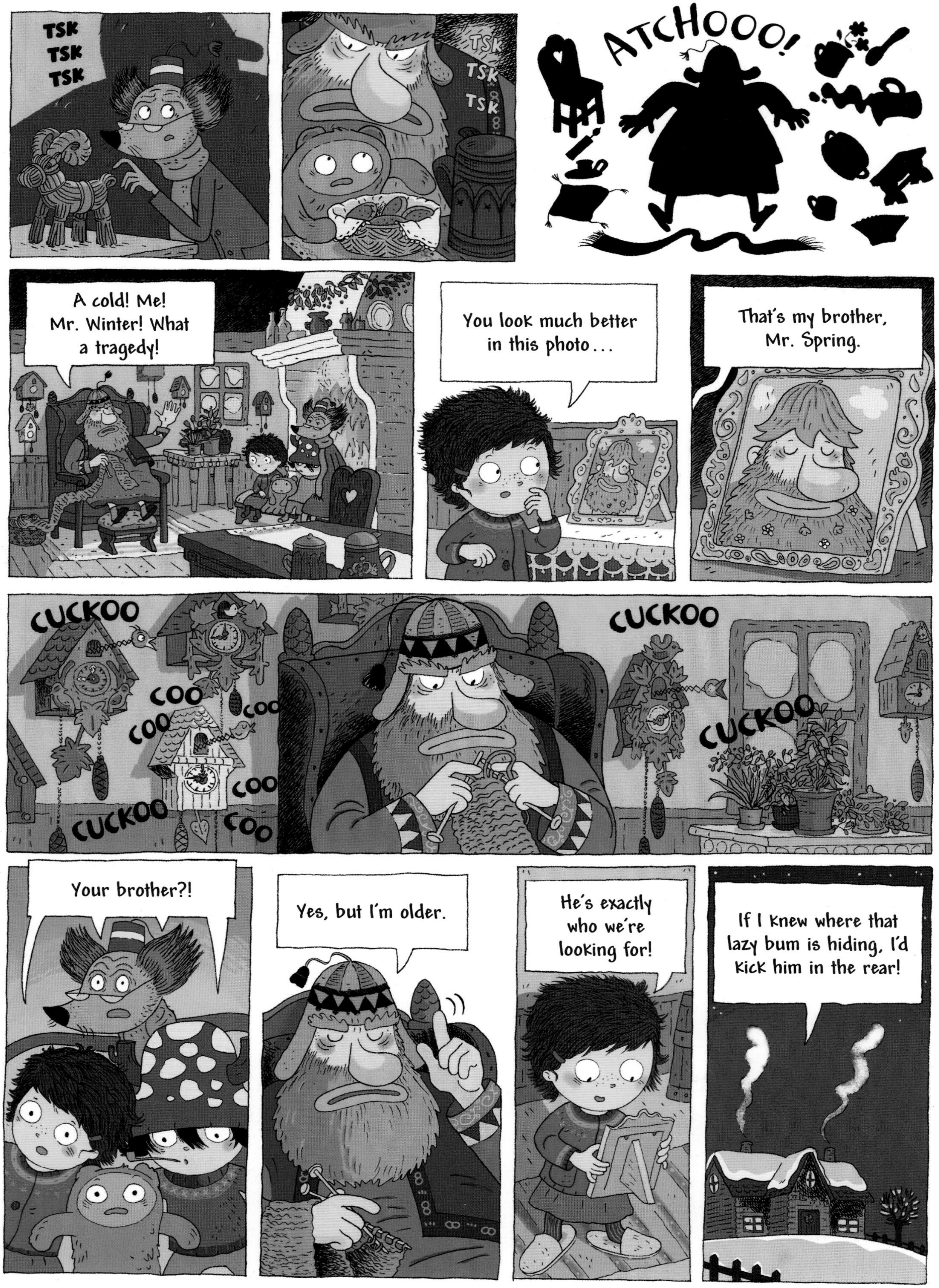
TSK
TSK
TSK
TSK
TSK
TSK
ATCHOOO!
A cold! Me! Mr. Winter! What a tragedy!
You look much better in this photo...
That's my brother, Mr. Spring.
CUCKOO
COO
COO
COO
COO
CUCKOO
COO
CUCKOO
CUCKOO
Your brother?!
Yes, but I'm older.
He's exactly who we're looking for!
If I knew where that lazy bum is hiding, I'd kick him in the rear!

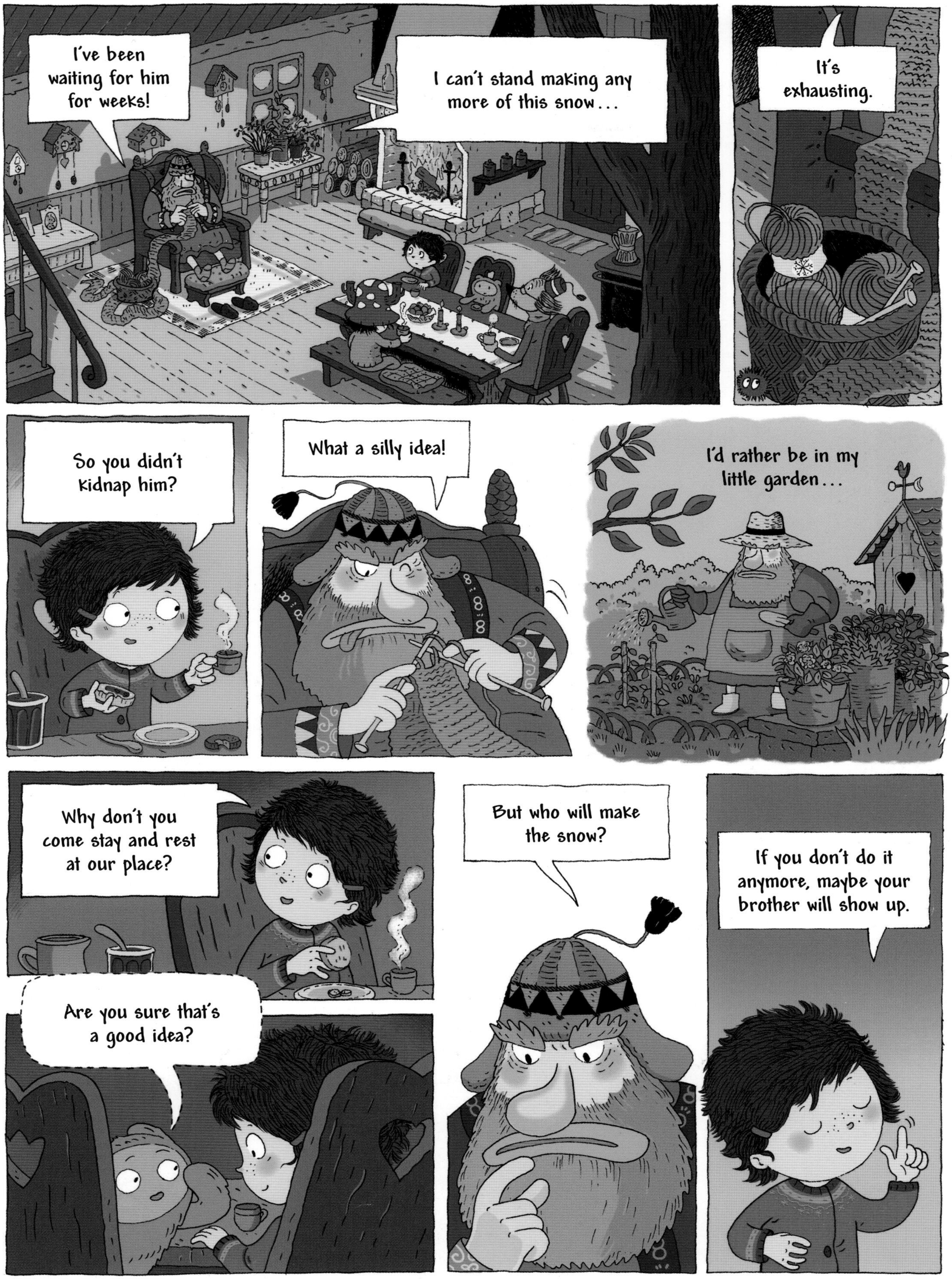
I've been waiting for him for weeks!
I can't stand making any more of this snow...
It's exhausting.
So you didn't kidnap him?
What a silly idea!
I'd rather be in my little garden...
Why don't you come stay and rest at our place?
Are you sure that's a good idea?
But who will make the snow?
If you don't do it anymore, maybe your brother will show up.

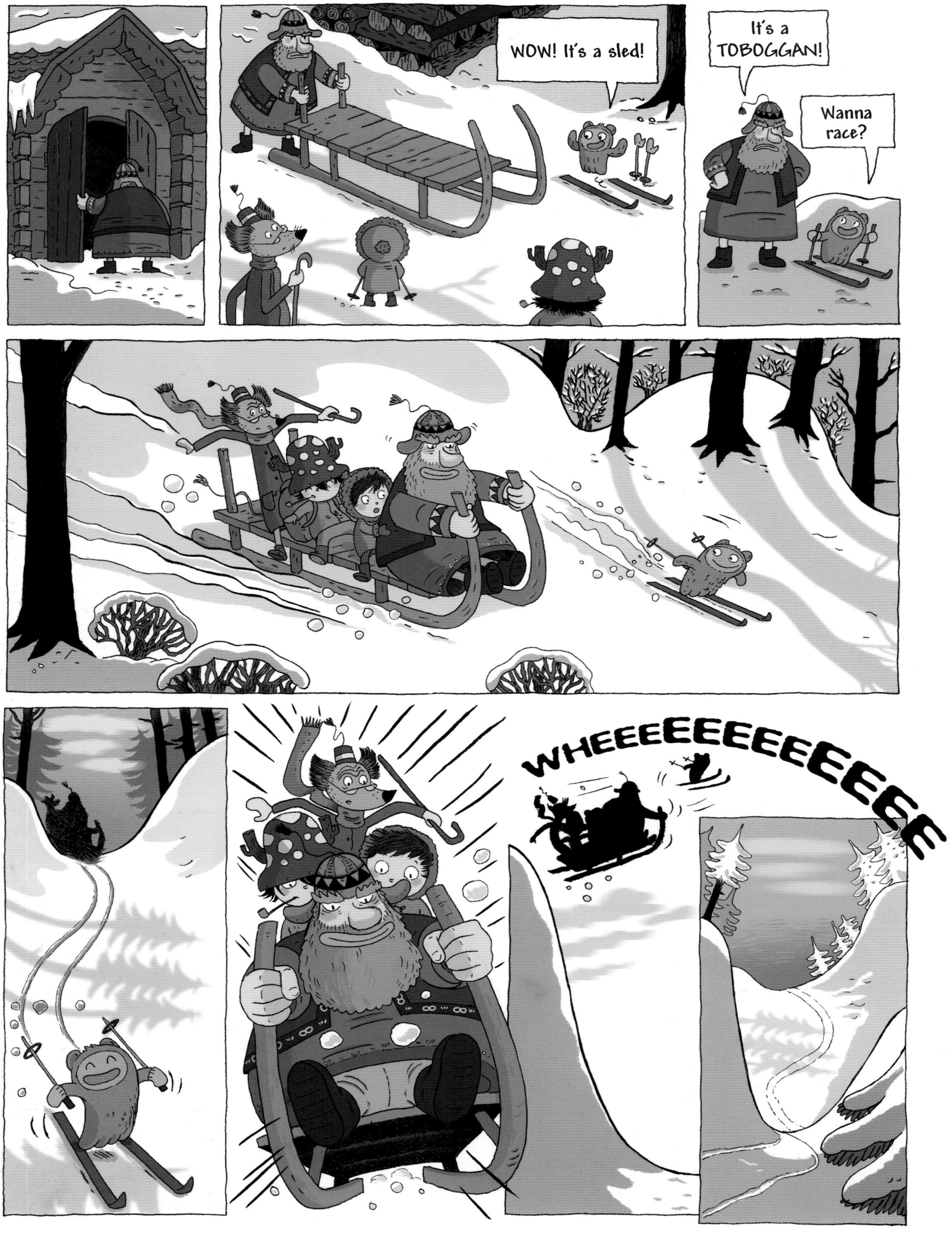

WOW! It's a sled!
It's a TOBOGGAN!
Wanna race?
WHEEEEEEEEEEEEEE

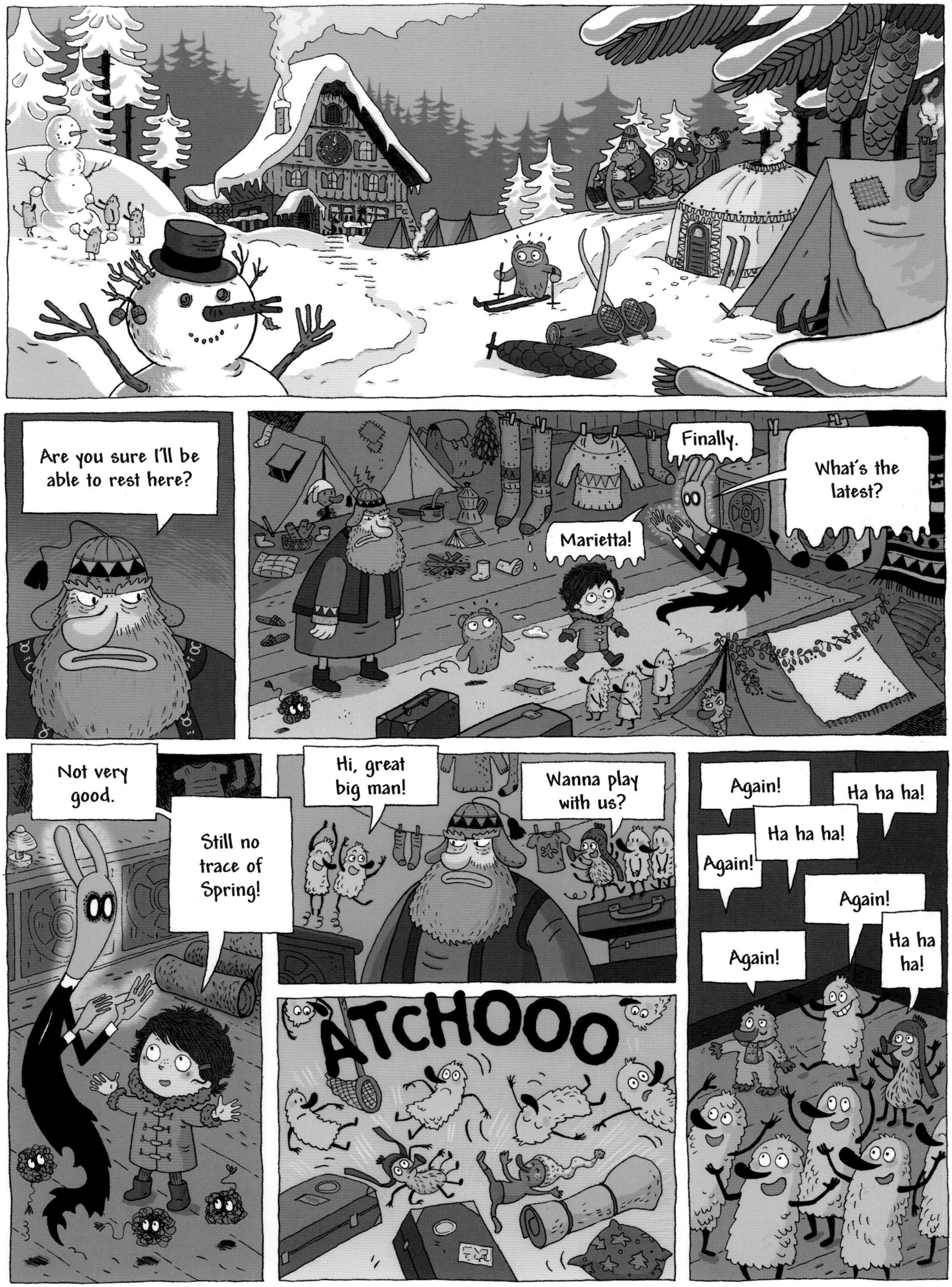
Are you sure I'll be able to rest here?
Finally.
What's the latest?
Marietta!
Not very good.
Still no trace of Spring!
Hi, great big man!
Wanna play with us?
ATCHOOO
Again!
Ha ha ha!
Ha ha ha!
Again!
Again!
Again!
Ha ha ha!

I wanted to fish!

I wanted to hike!

Look at the garden!

I'm so hungry!

I want my money back!

Kiki, go see what's left in the cellar.

I'll slip off to the kitchen.

NO WAY!

I'm not going down there with all the blood slurpers!

In the cellar?

Impossible! The blood slurpers only hibernate in the attic.

grumble grumble grumble

See?

What else could that be?

ROOO

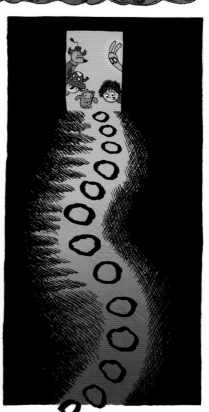

ROOOO

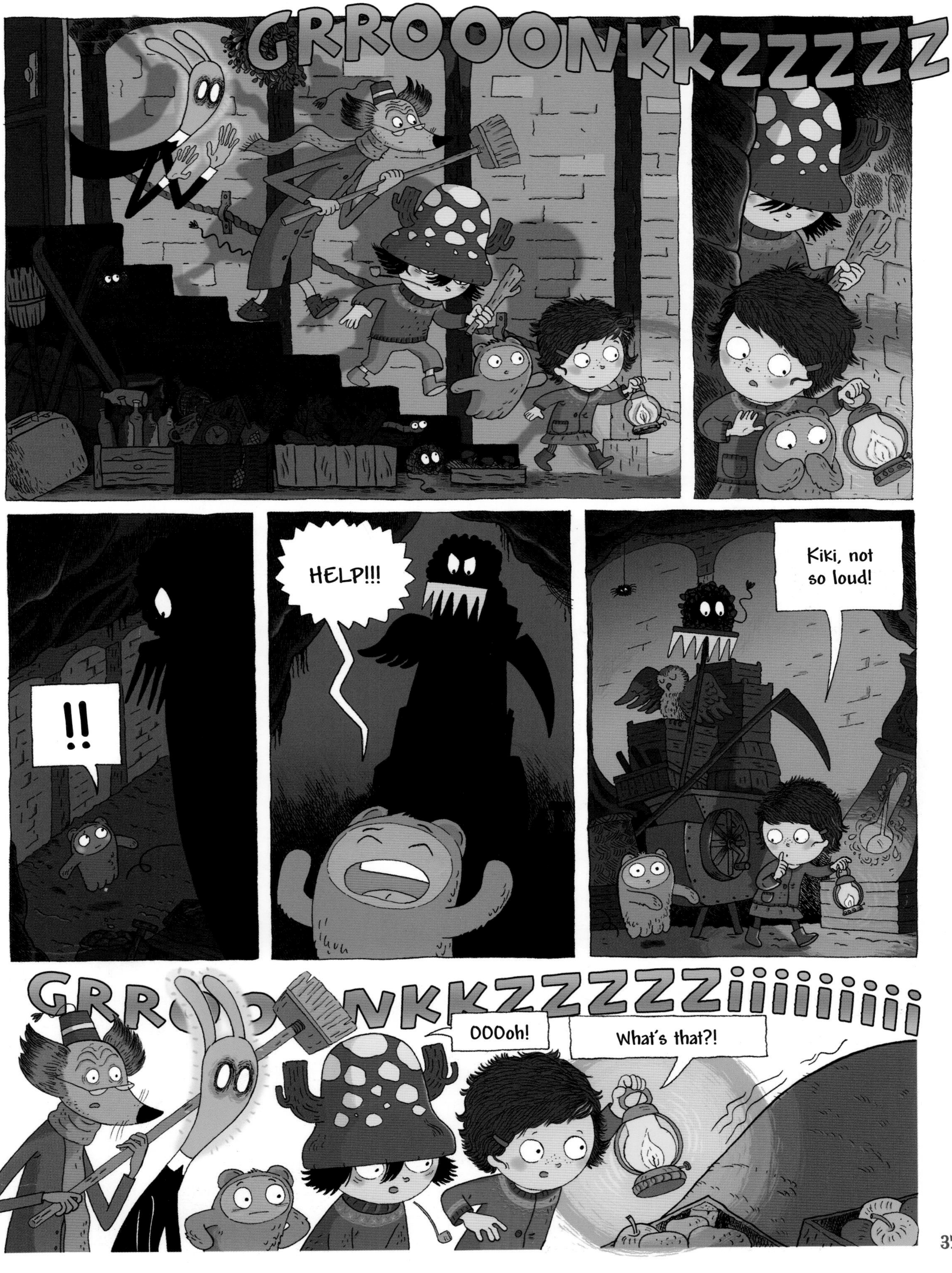
GRROOONKKZZZZZ
!!
HELP!!!
Kiki, not so loud!
GRROOONKKZZZZZiiiiiiiii
OOOoh!
What's that?!

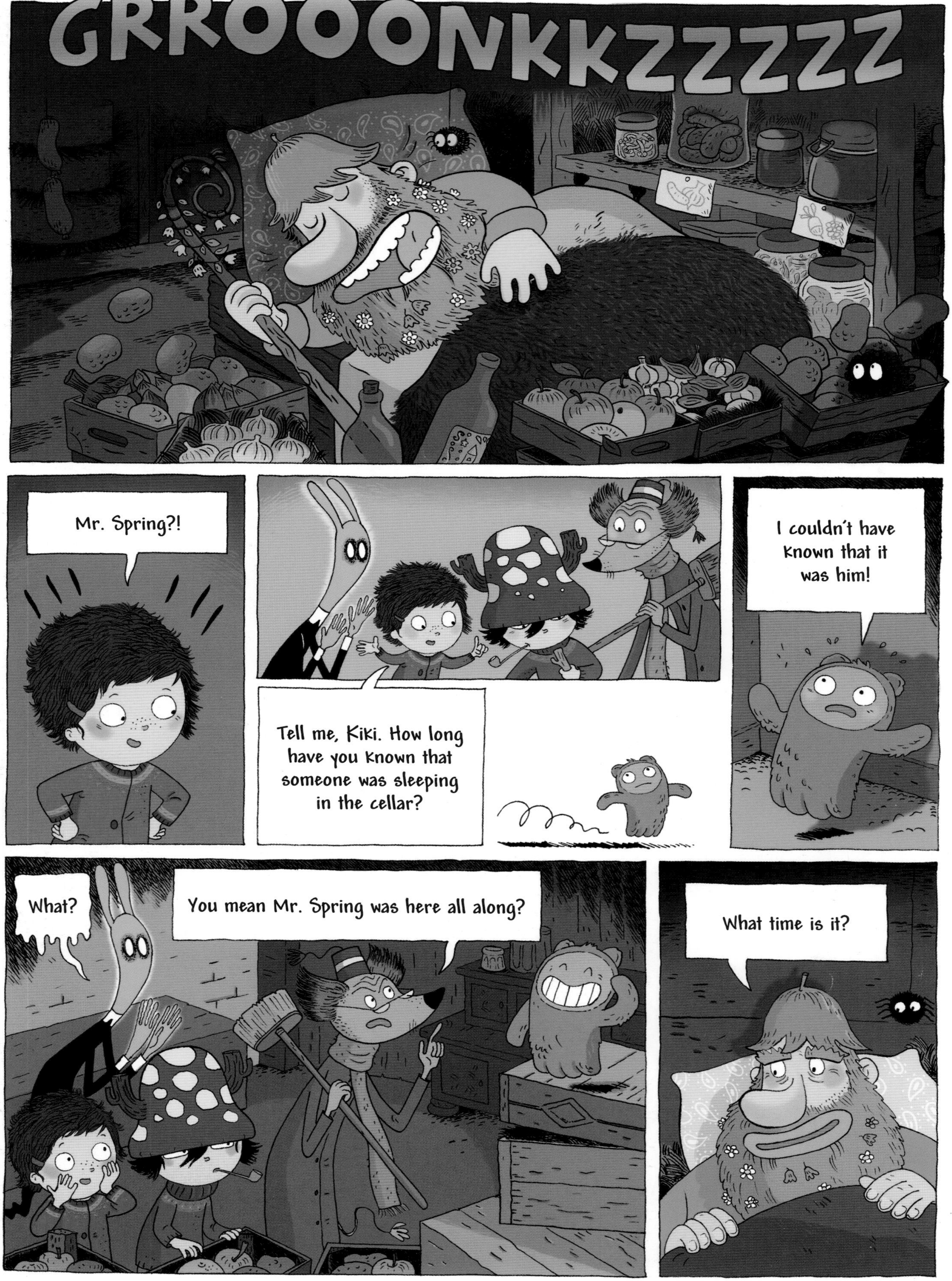
GRROOONKKZZZZZ
Mr. Spring?!
Tell me, Kiki. How long have you known that someone was sleeping in the cellar?
I couldn't have known that it was him!
What?
You mean Mr. Spring was here all along?
What time is it?

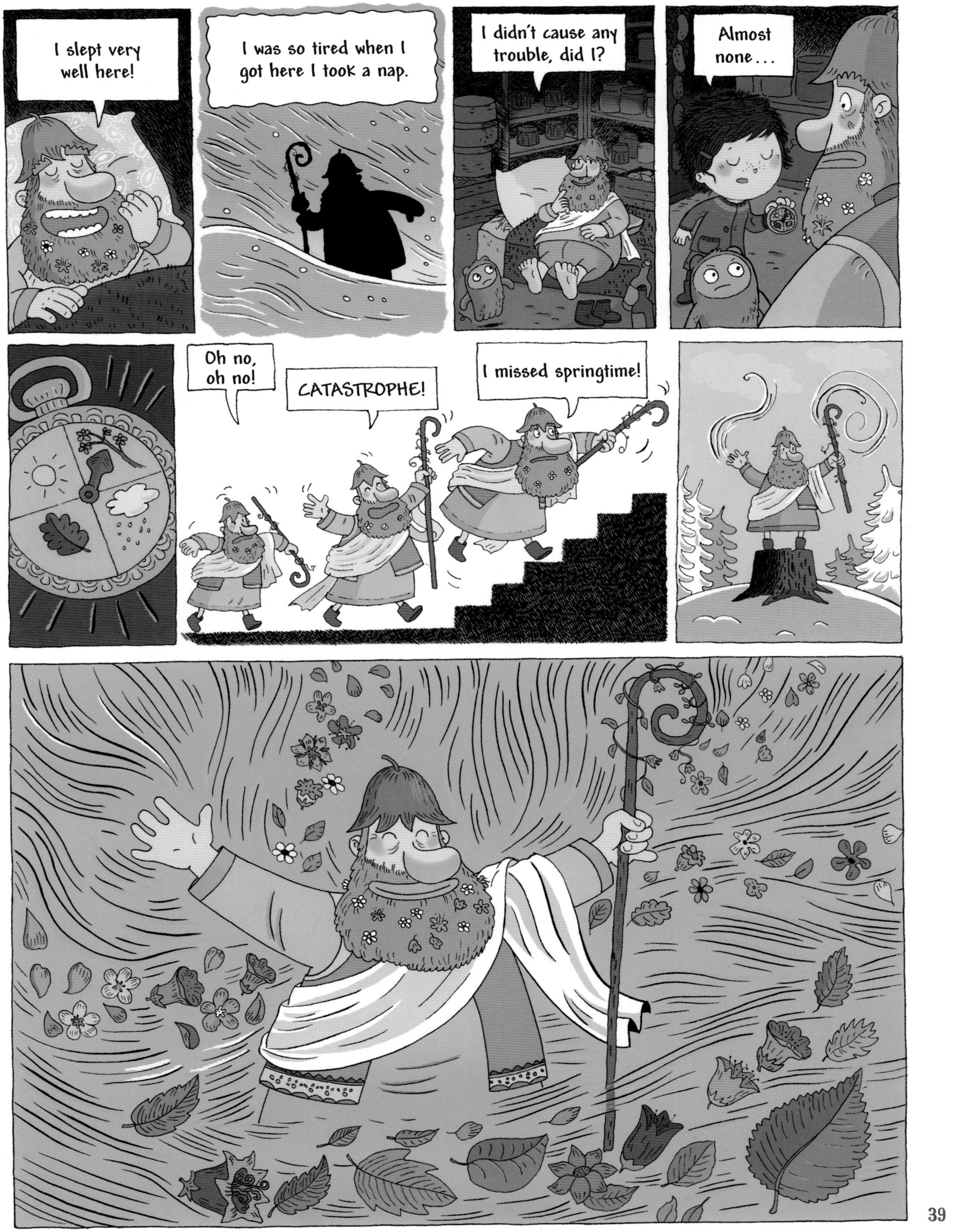
I slept very well here!
I was so tired when I got here I took a nap.
I didn't cause any trouble, did I?
Almost none...
Oh no, oh no!
CATASTROPHE!
I missed springtime!

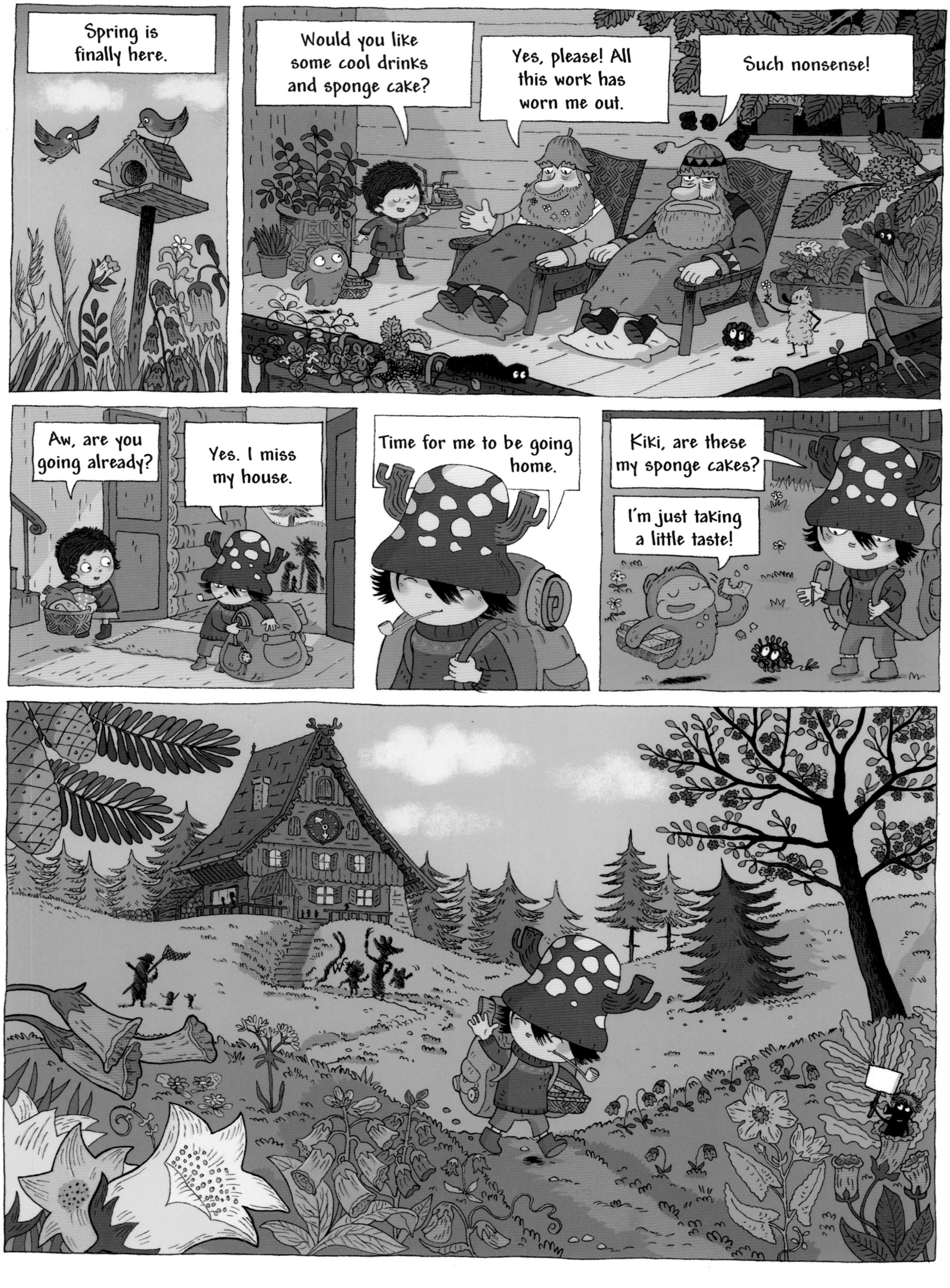
Spring is finally here.
Would you like some cool drinks and sponge cake?
Yes, please! All this work has worn me out.
Such nonsense!
Aw, are you going already?
Yes. I miss my house.
Time for me to be going home.
Kiki, are these my sponge cakes?
I'm just taking a little taste!

Sponge Cake

Ask an adult for help in the kitchen.

7 tablespoons butter
½ cup flour
¾ cup granulated sugar
½ cup almond meal (also known as almond flour)
1 pinch salt
4 egg whites

preparation time: 15 minutes
cooking time: 20 to 25 minutes

1. Preheat the oven to 350°F. Line the cups of a standard 12-cup muffin pan with paper liners.
2. Melt butter in a small pan until it just starts to brown, approximately 3 to 5 minutes. Let cool.
3. Stir together flour, sugar, almond meal, and salt.
4. Use a hand mixer or a stand mixer to beat butter and egg whites into the flour mixture. Beat for 1 to 2 minutes to fully blend the ingredients.
5. Divide the mixture evenly among the prepared muffin cups—filling them one-half to three-quarters full. Place the muffin pan in the oven. Let cook 20 to 25 minutes until the sponge cakes have browned.
6. Let the sponge cakes cool slightly, 1 to 2 minutes. Then gently turn them out of the pans and let them cool the rest of the way on a cooling rack.

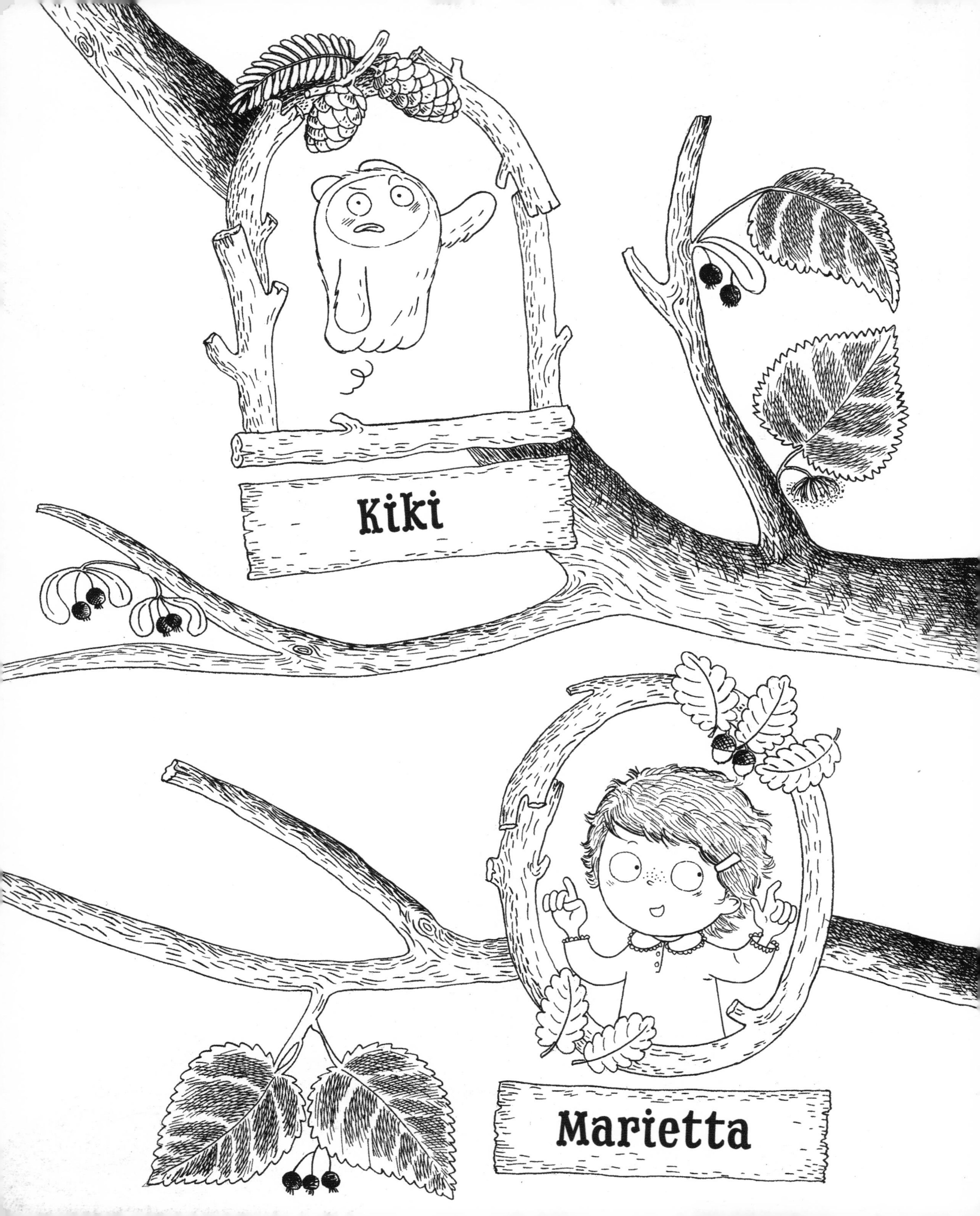
Kiki
Marietta

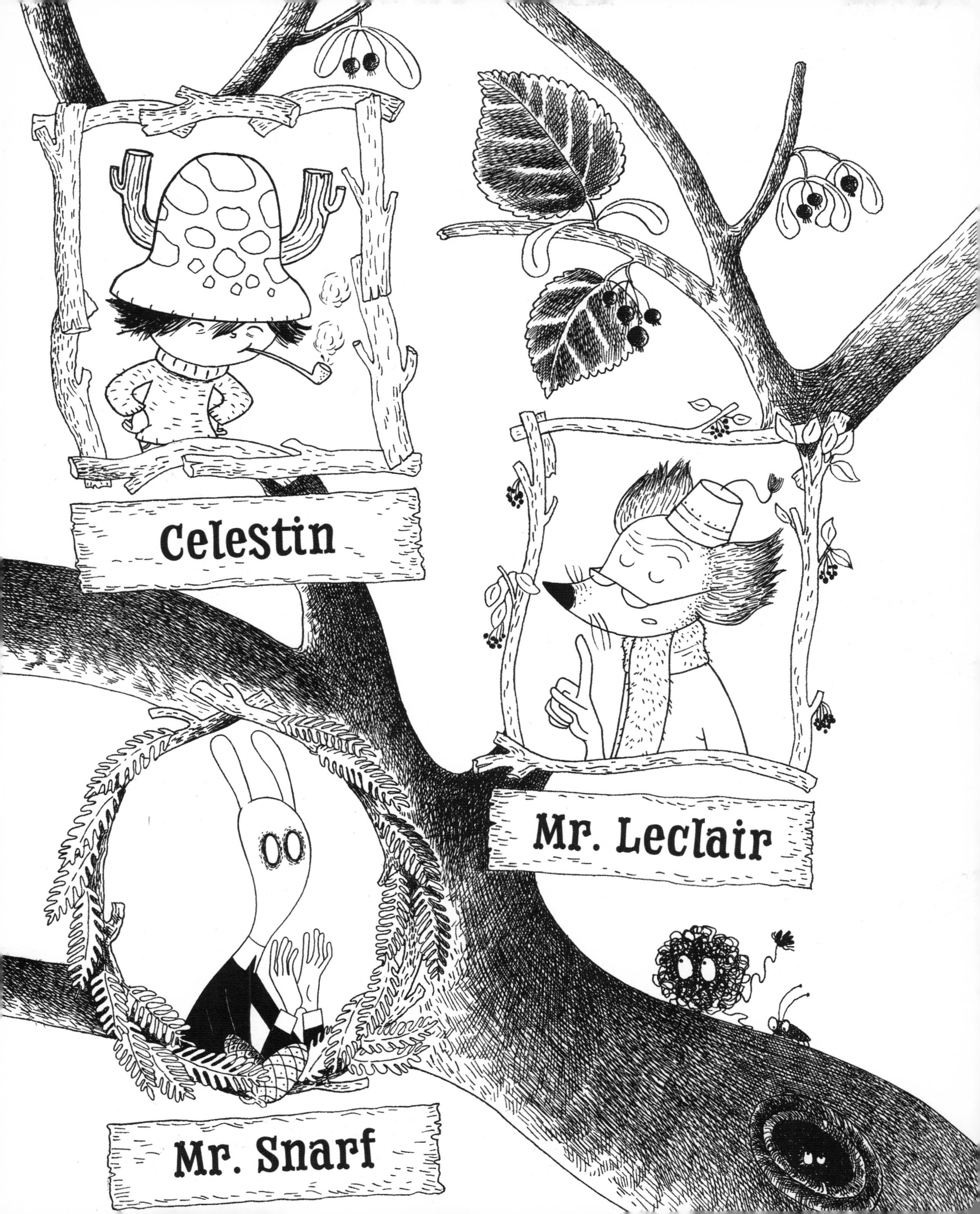
Celestin
Mr. Leclair
Mr. Snarf